STEPPING UP

The Bully in the Band

a richer, fuller
life through music.

Ann Kingston
Paul [illegible]

Stepping Up:
The Bully in the Band

Dale's concentration was broken when Jim leaned over and whispered, "I can't wait to watch you clutch like you did at your auditions. You do remember you messed up two different times. Get ready for mess up numbers three and four."

Dale realized that it was the time to take on Jim. As Jim turned forward, Dale leaned over, reached into his shirt, pulling out Scout's two dog tags that he always wore on a chain around his neck.

"I don't think so, Jim. I know what you did and how you did it. Does this look familiar?" Dale said as he held up a pink eraser dangling on the chain with the dog tags. Jim's face turned white. "I think, Jim, it's time I erased the past and show you what a real leader plays like."

Book Four

STEPPING UP

THE BULLY IN THE BAND

PAUL KIMPTON

AND

ANN KACZKOWSKI KIMPTON

GIA Publications, Inc.
Chicago

Stepping Up: The Bully in the Band

Paul Kimpton and Ann Kaczkowski Kimpton

Book design and layout by Martha Chlipala

GIA Publications, Inc.
7404 S Mason Ave
Chicago IL 60638
www.giamusic.com

G-8925
ISBN: 978-1-62277-141-7

For our parents who instilled in us a love
of music,
the outdoors,
and adventure.

For Dr. Carroll Gonzo, our wise GIA editor.
For Martha Chlipala's great illustration.

For the Adventures with Music Early Readers Club, and their suggestions.

For Karen Moffett and her band students
at Westview Middle School, Willowbrook, Illinois.

A special thanks to the Early Readers Club students Bradley William Davis, Ean Cassity, Elisabeth Bieber, V. Cole Merkin, Anna Gruchala, and Patrick Hsiao from Willowbrook, Illinois, and Callen Sell from Orlando, Florida, for all their suggestions.
For Julie Dorn, Youth Librarian at the Warren County Public Library, Monmouth, Illinois.

A special thanks to the Early Readers Club students Zane Tibbett – Zesbaugh, Talia Long, Jake Thomas, Ashlyn Kaye Quinn, Madeline Blaesing, Emmi Kay Frieden, and Grace Murk from Monmouth, Illinois, and Shannon Pierce and Brandon Martin from Raton, New Mexico, for all their suggestions.

Thanks to Byron Hanson, Archivist,
Interlochen *Center for the Arts, for the information and programs from 1933 to 1947.*

Thanks to the Chicago Symphony and its continuing support of exposing children to the arts in order to create future generations of musicians.

STEPPING UP

THE BULLY IN THE BAND

Chapter 1

The Train Trestle

Dale leaned back against the cool steel of the train trestle that crossed Dawson Lake. As his friends dangled their legs off the cement pylons of the bridge overlooking the choppy water, they shared stories of the past summer. The gang had made a pact to do twelve things when they all turned twelve. For their final group activity, Bobby suggested they meet at the train trestle, which he said was no longer in use by the railroad. The group of ten climbed onto the supporting cross bars of the trestle to the center pylon, where they could laze in the warm sun and share one last adventure together before school started. It was the final day of summer vacation—Labor Day, September 3, 1945—just two weeks since the war with Japan ended.

Dave was the first to share his initial adventure. He pretended to row furiously, swinging his body to the left, demonstrating an Eskimo roll in his kayak. Bridget screamed and grabbed Dave, thinking he was about to fall, but Dave just laughed, and finished his story about almost drowning before he could turn upright. Karl pretended to take the reins and gallop when he told about getting thrown off a horse named Sugar, who was anything but sweet. Thankfully, the girls stopped Karl from showing them the saddle sores he still had from all the horseback riding he had done. Chrissy was the last to go, and told the story of how she and Dale learned to shoot clay pigeons, or skeet, with a shotgun. Dale didn't interrupt her story, although he still believed he hit more than she did.

"Dale, do you want to add anything to my story about shooting skeet?"

"I do have to say after listening to everyone's stories about their 'first' lists that this has been one great summer. Now, if I can only catch a big channel catfish, I'll have finished all my firsts." Dale grabbed his fishing pole, which was leaning against the bridge, and cast the pole's line into the lake.

Victor looked at Dale with a skeptical eye. "I still don't see how you're going to pull a big catfish all the way up here. We must be a good two stories above the water."

Dale remained confident. "I'll worry about that when I catch it. If there's a will, there's a way."

"I hate to interrupt this discussion of fishing, but I brought something from our trip to Chicago and the Ravinia concert that I want to share with everyone," Chrissy said as she opened her backpack. "I hope you like it," and she pulled out a package covered with brown wrapping paper.

"Come on, Chrissy, enough of the suspense!" P.J. said as he pushed in next to his friend.

Chrissy tore off the paper, revealing a rectangular photo album with a title written in cursive on the front.

Summer of Firsts Trip to Chicago:
An Adventure to Remember

Bridget let out a scream of excitement and Sandra inched forward on the cement. "Don't tell me these are the pictures from our trip. I forgot all about you and your camera."

Chrissy proudly opened the album. "These aren't just photos. I made a scrapbook with everything from our trip. She pointed out the page with the itinerary their band director, Mr. Jeffrey, had given them, and the ticket stub and program from the Ravinia concert by the Chicago Symphony. Under each piece of memorabilia and/or photograph, Chrissy had printed a short description.

"I wish you had a picture of how we climbed out on this trestle just now," Bridget said nervously as she glanced down at the water. That would prove that I actually completed the last group event without getting hurt."

"Don't pat yourself on the back yet," Bobby pointed out. "You still have to climb all the way back before you can say you finished your list."

"Thanks for ruining a great feeling," she said stoically as she maneuvered herself closer to the center to refocus on the album. Dale, not getting any bites on his line, moved over to the other side of the pylon and casted closer to a tree that had fallen into the water.

Chrissy turned the pages, enjoying her friends' approval of her album. Dave and Tommy loved the picture of Officer O'Brien pretending to arrest Dale and P.J. when they stood under the two bronze lions that guarded the main entrance of the Art Institute. Sandra liked the photo of the group planting their feet in Lake Michigan, with the girls riding on the backs of the boys. P.J. thought the group photo that included Mr. and Mrs. Capitanini, owners of the Italian Village restaurant, was the best. Bobby liked the picture of his friends lying in the grass at Ravinia before the concert, eating the sausages, cheese, and cannoli that Mrs. Capitanini had packed. As they neared the end of the album, Chrissy abruptly put her hand on the page. "I hope you like these last few photographs. I took them when you weren't paying attention. They are random shots of us doing, well … you'll see."

The group burst out laughing as she turned the page. There was P.J., running toward the train after the Ravinia concert, his shirt hanging out, his mouth open, and sweat running down his face. Pulling him by the arm was the tuba player from the Chicago Symphony, Arnold Jacobs.

"I don't see what's so funny about that picture," P.J. said defensively.

"Of course you don't think it's funny, but if you think about how you almost missed the train, and the look of terror on your face, then it really is funny." Chrissy gave P.J. a soft but friendly punch in the shoulder. "Come on, relax."

"OK, I do have to admit it's funny, but I wish I had a picture of your faces looking out the window at me."

"No problem," said Chrissy. She turned the page to the next photograph of the gang with their faces pressed against the train window—a spectacle of impish onlookers that brought another round of laughter.

One final photograph told the entire story. There stood the gang with their parents on the platform at the Libertyville station after their triumphal return from Chicago at four in the morning. Dale, whose face and overalls were covered in black soot from riding in the engine with his grandfather, was front and center shaking Mr. Jeffrey's hand.

Sandra said softly, "Look at how excited we are after all that happened, and do you see Dale's face? He looks like a raccoon with those white circles around his eyes where his goggles were." While looking at the picture, there was a commotion because Dale felt a firm tug on his line. He stood up and yanked back to set the hook. "Got one!" The gang peered over the edge to see the fish flip out of the water, fighting to get off the hook.

Chrissy shouted encouragement: "Remember, if you catch this fish, you'll finish your list."

With his friends cheering, Dale slowly turned the reel and pulled back on the pole. The fish continued to swim from side to side, its fin cutting a path through the water, resisting the line that was irrevocably pulling him through the water toward the pylon and an uncertain future. Victor shook his head stoically. "I don't see how you're going to get that fish up here. You'd better figure out another way."

"The only other way I can land this fish is to climb up on the trestle and then work my way down the tracks to the bank. Then, I'll try to land it from the shore. I don't see any other way."

Sandra interrupted. "I don't think that sounds like a good idea. What if you trip and fall off the trestle, or worse, a train comes? Just cut the fish loose, and play it safe."

Bobby was perturbed. "I told you these tracks are abandoned. Plus, Dale's a great climber with super balance." He stood up and reached for the pole. "Dale, climb up on the tracks, and I'll pass the rod up to you."

The girls, racked with fear, stood with their hands over their mouths while Dale passed the pole to Bobby and hoisted himself up with ease onto the top of the trestle. "OK, Bobby, pass the pole up. Be sure to keep tension on the line or the fish will spit out the hook, and I'll lose it!" Bobby carefully passed the pole to Dale who grabbed it with two hands. The fish still wriggled violently in the water below. As Dale turned to edge his way down the tracks, the sound of a whistle pierced the air.

"What was that?" Bridget shouted as she glanced up at Dale.

Bobby scoffed at the girl's concern. "There are train tracks close by. I did the research, and I know these tracks are not in use."

"I hope you're right," Victor said skeptically as he looked up at the rails. "I still say the train tracks seemed a bit shiny when we walked down them this morning." In the distance, the whistle sounded again. This time it was louder than before.

Bobby's earlier confidence was beginning to fade, prompting him to vigorously urge Dale to get moving and land that fish.

Dale slowly stepped from one railroad tie to the next, keeping his pole high in the air so as not to lose the fish.

Chrissy glanced at Bobby and shouted frantically, "Hurry up! Not that Bobby could ever be wrong...."

Dale was determined to land this fish. "I can only go so fast, if I want to keep my balance."

Bobby put his hand against the steel beam of the trestle. He leaned toward Bridget and whispered, "Do you feel something?"

"Feel what?"

"Put your hand on the metal. I think I feel a vibration from the rails above." He stepped backwards, almost knocking Tommy into the water. "How could I have been wrong?"

"Who cares if you're wrong?" Tommy exhorted. "We have to get Dale off the bridge before the train comes."

Chrissy screamed with fright and pointed down the track at a puff of smoke in the distance. Dale turned to see what was causing the excitement. At the bend in the tracks about a half mile away, a steam engine bellowing black smoke chugged down the tracks leading to the trestle. Dale was in the middle of the span over the deepest part of Dawson Lake and had to make a choice. He either had to take a chance that he could get to the end of the bridge before the train, or he could drop the fishing pole and climb back down under the tracks, letting the train pass over him. Another possibility was to jump into the water.

The sound of the steam engine rumbling toward him and the whistle's scream blocked out the words of his friends. Still holding the fishing pole, Dale began to run along the ties toward the end of the bridge.

His friends watched in horror as they realized that Dale couldn't beat the train and get off the bridge. Dale came to the same conclusion while periodically glancing at the approaching engine. The train was so close that he could see the engineer leaning out the window waving his arms for the boy to get off the bridge.

Dale made his choice. He put his legs together with the pole wrapped in his arms across his chest and jumped feet first off the trestle just as the steam engine began crossing the bridge. Dale hit the water as the train thundered across the trestle above. The gang anxiously peered over the edge. The tracks shook as train car after train car passed directly over their heads. All eyes were on the water where Dale had landed, but they saw nothing except the rings of the waves caused by Dale entering the water. The caboose crossed the bridge, and the group could finally hear each other's voices. P.J. and Tommy shouted Dale's name from the trestle.

"Bobby, if anything happens to Dale because of your bright idea about this bridge and it being abandoned...well, I don't know what I'll do, but it won't be nice." Bridget, agitated, took a threatening step toward Bobby.

Victor was the first to spy the tip of the pole bobbing to the surface, followed by Dale holding onto it with one hand while he treaded water.

Dale shook the water from his face and yelled up to his friends who looked down in amazement. "I made it and still have the fish! YEE HAW!"

Sandra cupped her hands and yelled down, "Swim to the bank before you drown!" And with a commanding voice she added, "Let that stupid fish go!"

"There's no way after jumping off that bridge with this fish that I'm letting go," he said as he swam toward the shore using his free arm.

Dale staggered onto the bank and began to reel in his prize. A few minutes later, Dale reeled in a huge gray channel catfish onto the lake's bank.

The gang began chanting Dale's name from the bridge trestle. Dale admired his catch and held it high for the gang to see. "Get over here. We've had enough excitement for the day and maybe for a lifetime."

One by one, they climbed under the trestle to the safety of the shore and slipped down the bank to Dale. Bobby was the last to arrive. He slumped to the ground, holding his head in his hands. "I thought it was abandoned; I thought it was abandoned."

Chrissy, Bridget, and Sandra gave Dale a hug, while P.J. pulled up the line to test the weight of the huge catfish.

"I think we've had one heck of an ending to our summer of firsts," Dale said as he walked over to Bobby. "That's OK, Bobby, we forgive you. I'm fine, and we know you didn't do this on purpose. Let's shake hands. Agreed?" Dale turned to his friends.

"Agreed!" the group replied. They followed Dale's lead, and each in turn shook hands with Bobby.

Dale turned to climb up the bank. "Let's get going, so I can get this fish home before it starts to smell." During the walk back to their bikes, Dale urged his friends to make a promise.

"I want everyone to swear that you will not tell your parents about me jumping off that bridge. Can you imagine the trouble I would be in? It's our secret. Agreed?"

"I'll agree only if we can talk about it when we are together because that was the greatest group event of a lifetime, and I don't want to forget it," Victor said.

Dale nodded. "We can only talk when we're together. Agreed?"

Everyone replied, "Agreed."

During the walk down the tracks to get to their bikes, the gang kept looking over their shoulders for the next train, but luckily none came.

"Chrissy, I wish you had your camera to get this shot of us all riding back with me carrying the catch of a lifetime on my shoulder."

"I have a mental picture of what happened today. But what I'm really looking forward to are the adventures we're going to have. It all begins tomorrow when we start junior high."

"You might be right that the best is yet to come, but I hope it doesn't involve me jumping off any more bridges!"

One by one, the friends dropped each other off at their respective houses until it was only Chrissy and Dale riding up Simpson Hill.

"I am really glad nothing terrible happened to you today. I was so scared."

"Thanks, Chris. I will never let anything happen to...."

As they came over the crest of the hill, Chrissy stopped abruptly. "Look. If I'm not mistaken, don't your grandparents and mom look angry standing on the porch with their arms crossed? You don't think they found out about the bridge, do you?"

Dale swallowed and replied, "Nothing happens in Libertyville that my grandmother doesn't know. Maybe you

should ride to your house alone, and I'll face them myself."
And with that, Chrissy took off pedaling as fast as she could.

Chapter 2

NEWS TRAVELS FAST

Dale hadn't planned to exercise before his first day of school at East Libertyville Junior High, but with all the excitement from the day before, he needed to clear his head. The cool morning temperature felt good on his sweaty face as he ran up Simpson Hill for the second time, his dog Scout galloping by his side. Once he reached the top, he paused to catch his breath while Scout panted, his tongue dripping saliva on the pavement.

Dale knelt and patted the dog. "I hope you don't mind that you can't go to the fire station to spend the day with Smokey like you used to when I went to Emerson Grade School." Scout turned his head side to side as if trying to understand Dale's words. Then Dale heard a familiar voice. He turned and saw

Mr. Valentine, the milkman, coming out of the alley. He was in his milk wagon being pulled by his horse, Buddy. They had just finished the milk deliveries on Dale's block.

The horse-drawn wagon pulled alongside Dale and Scout, and Mr. Valentine leaned out.

"Sounds like you had a little excitement yesterday from what I hear."

Dale paused, and then asked, "What do you mean?"

"It isn't every day that someone has to jump off a bridge to land a catfish. I'm just glad you're OK."

"I'm fine, but how did you find out?"

Mr. Valentine chuckled. "Nothing happens in Libertyville that I don't know about. Each morning on my route, I hear the latest news from my customers. I even heard that your punishment is that you are grounded and must wash all the windows on the outside of your house."

Dale looked up sheepishly at Mr. Valentine and added, "And you know my grandma … she'll continue to remind me about taking foolish risks the whole time I'm grounded. But, at least I finished my list by catching that fish. I just wish it hadn't been so scary."

"Here, give Buddy this carrot so you can get back to your exercise, and I can get back to my route. I have to say you look taller and stronger as a result of your summer workouts."

"Really?" Dale puffed out his chest and stood as tall as he could.

"Now, get going so you're not late for your first day of school."

Mr. Valentine's comment jogged Dale back to reality and he took off running toward his house with Scout giving chase. *What will my first day of junior high be like?*

Mrs. Smith, Dale's neighbor, came out to get her milk from the porch. She called to Dale and asked if he was OK and if he had eaten the channel cat for dinner. News does travel fast, he thought as he ran through the yard to his back door. He was greeted by the smell of coffee, and sausages and eggs on the skillet.

"Well, well, if it isn't Mr. Daredevil himself," his grandfather said, lowering the morning paper.

"Morning, Grandpa. Sorry about yesterday. You wouldn't believe that even Mr. Valentine knew."

"I am sure he did. Now don't forget that after school you have to come home right away and wash windows."

Dale nodded reluctantly and began shoveling eggs into his mouth.

Grandma set a hot cup of coffee with cream in front of Dale. "All I have to say is I'm glad you didn't hurt yourself. If any good came from yesterday, it might have been that you finished that darned list and learned a good lesson about taking risks." Dale looked sheepishly at his grandmother. "I must admit that it was one of the best fish we've eaten for some time," and she broke into a smile. "But enough of yesterday. Are you excited about your first day as a seventh grader?"

Dale took a sip of his coffee. "Well, yes and no," he admitted. "I'm excited about going to a new school and meeting new kids, but I'm a little nervous about having to go from class to class in five minutes. The school is so big and has so many stairways and halls. I hope I don't get lost."

"Don't worry. You've been to that school numerous times for band. Remember, you have all your band friends and classmates from Emerson School who'll be with you. They all will be in the same boat as you, trying to navigate their first day."

Dale admitted that Grandma was right. "I shouldn't think so much. That reminds me, where's Mom this morning? I didn't hear her leave."

Grandpa winked at Grandma. "After you went to bed, she left late last night, saying she had an important mission to fly. Something about having to pick up a top-secret package and fly it back to Libertyville today." Dale's mother was finishing up her service with the WASPs, an acronym for Women's Air Force Service Pilots.

"Top secret? What does that mean? I thought the war was over."

"You're right. The war is officially over. While you were jumping off the bridge, the Japanese representatives on the battleship Missouri in Tokyo Bay signed the official documents. Look, here's a picture of the signing on the front page in today's newspaper."

Dale took the paper from his grandfather and scanned the story. "So, even after the Japanese surrendered on August 15, they still had to sign an official agreement?"

"They sure did. The document detailed how the Japanese would rebuild their country and what they could and couldn't do. This is a very big moment in history, and it will be remembered as 'VJ Day': Victory Over Japan. I hope you'll remember it."

"There's no way I'll ever forget September 3, 1945," Dale said confidently.

"Why is that?"

"That's easy. It's the same day I jumped off a bridge and caught the biggest fish of my life."

Grandpa laughed and looked up. Grandma was frowning. "Don't encourage him, C.H. Now go get ready for your first day as a seventh grader." Before Dale could race up the stairs to his room, Grandma added, "And don't forget your punishment. I'll have the rags and bucket ready for you."

"I won't," Dale said, thinking about what his grandmother said earlier. *A secret mission ... now what could that be?*

Chapter 3

FIRST DAY

Dale sat on the front porch steps waiting for Chrissy, with Scout by his side. Dale reminded Scout, "Today you have to stay here," but before he could finish, Scout bolted down the steps and across the street, as Chrissy came down her front steps.

Chrissy knelt to scratch Scout's belly. "Who's the good dog? Who's the good dog?" Scout wriggled on his back in delight.

Chrissy stood and shouted to Dale from the sidewalk. "Let's go! We have to pick up the rest of the gang to walk to school." She smiled broadly and twirled around on the sidewalk, her dress billowing in the wind.

Dale walked toward her and said admiringly, "You sure are all dressed up. You look so much older. It must be because you're a seventh-grade girl now and not some elementary tomboy."

Chrissy playfully punched Dale softly in the shoulder. "Thanks. My mom made my dress ... but remember, I can still outrun you most of the time."

"Maybe, but not with that fancy dress and those dress shoes on you won't."

Chrissy blushed. Dale turned and took Scout back to the front porch and commanded. "Stay, and don't follow me. Now get under the porch, and I'll see you after school." Scout's ears flattened, and his tail went between his legs, as he slowly followed Dale's commands and crawled under the porch.

Chrissy had already begun walking down the sidewalk, so Dale had to run to catch her.

Turning toward her friend, Chrissy said, "I think you're getting faster, and if I didn't know better, you look taller and stronger than you did in sixth grade. It must be all that exercise I see you doing in the morning."

Dale smiled to himself, feeling proud that Chrissy had noticed and that perhaps his hard work this summer was beginning to pay off.

The two walked toward East Libertyville Junior High in silence for the next several blocks. Finally, Chrissy spoke up. "How come you're so quiet this morning? It's not like you not to have something to say."

"I guess I'm a little nervous about my first day at East. With all the excitement yesterday, I haven't had time to really prepare."

"Don't be nervous. Remember, today only the seventh graders will be going through their schedules. There won't be any older kids until tomorrow. Besides, if I'm not nervous, you can't be," she said over her shoulder as she ran to meet Victor, Bobby, Bridget, and Dave, who were waiting on the corner. When Dale caught up to them, they were talking excitedly.

"What's happening?" Dale asked.

"We were telling Chrissy that our parents found out about yesterday and what you did. We didn't tell them ... they just found out. Plus, they weren't very happy that we had climbed out on the bridge. At least we're not grounded and have to wash windows like you."

"I have a feeling I am going to hear about this all day."

"Dale, Dale," P.J. shouted with Sandra, Tommy, and Karl running behind him. "They know," P.J. panted. "They know! My parents know! I didn't say a word, I promise ... they just knew."

"All our parents know," Sandra added, catching up to the group.

"I guess we can forget about agreeing not to talk about yesterday," Dale admitted. "Let's get going so we aren't late."

The gang continued the walk to school and was surprised by how many other kids were walking in the same direction. "I don't recognize anybody," Tommy said anxiously as he scanned the faces of a large group of students across the street. They must be from Wilson and Jackson."

Bridget picked up on Tommy's apprehension. "Where are all the Emerson kids?" she asked as she looked for a familiar face.

"Don't worry, they're here. These kids look friendly enough." Sandra's cool confidence prevailed, and the others followed her lead as they scurried up the steps to the junior high.

They entered the large doors that opened onto the foyer. Long wooden tables lined the opposite wall with large letters of the alphabet posted behind them.

"Welcome," said a tall man with short dark hair. "I'm Mr. Hamilton, the principal of East Liberty Junior High. Where are you from?"

Victor stepped forward, shaking Mr. Hamilton's hand. "We're all from Emerson."

"Emerson, hmm ... would one of you be Dale Kingston?"

The group backed away from Dale, thinking he was in trouble.

Dale slowly stepped forward, shaking Mr. Hamilton's hand. "I'm Dale Kingston. How do you know my name? I'm not in trouble, am I?"

Mr. Hamilton laughed. "No, you're not in trouble. I've heard all about your cornet playing and am looking forward to you helping our school win the state music contest that our sister school West Liberty has won the last ten years." He pointed to a glass trophy case behind the table. "Plus, I heard that you had an exciting last day of vacation and jumped off a bridge. Is that true?"

P.J. pushed forward to shake Mr. Hamilton's hand. "I'm P.J., and Dale not only jumped off the bridge, but he also caught a huge channel catfish."

"A channel cat! I love to fish. I'd like to hear about it sometime. It's great to meet you all. Now, what I want you to do is find the first letter of your last name," he said as he swept his arm toward the signs, "and get in that line. The guidance staff has your schedules and all the information you will need for the day." Mr. Hamilton then turned and went to meet the next group of students.

Dave was impressed that Mr. Hamilton had heard about Dale. "Once we all get our schedules, let's meet here by the stairs before we start the day. Agreed?"

"Agreed!" they answered as they moved to get in line.

"P.J., P.J., what are you doing," Sandra whispered when P.J. got in line with her. "Your last name doesn't begin with a J. Your last name is Walsh, so go and find the line for W."

P.J. blushed. "Thanks for saying something. I would have been really embarrassed. I'd better start using my real name Charlie Walsh and not my nickname P.J." He quickly changed lines.

After several minutes, Dale got to the front of the line. "Next! What's your name?" A dark-haired woman wearing horned-rimmed glasses snapped as Dale stepped forward.

"Dale Kingston, from Emerson School," Dale replied nervously.

The woman's facial expression went from frowning to smiling. "I know that name. Aren't you that cornet player I saw playing with the Andrews Sisters at the Air Force base last December?"

"Yes, ma'am, I am."

"Well, you were great. I hope you can help us get that state music trophy out of West Liberty's hands. I have your schedule in this packet and a map of the school to help guide you. Take this packet and go into the auditorium for a short speech by Principal Hamilton. Oh, and one more thing, I'm Miss Culver, your guidance counselor for the year. I hope you learned your lesson yesterday about taking unneeded risks. Now, off you go."

"Nice to meet you, and yes, I think I have learned my lesson." Dale turned and headed to the stairs to meet his friends.

As each friend arrived, they compared schedules before moving into the auditorium to find seats together.

"Do you believe that I only have band with you guys and gym with Victor?" Dale said looking at his schedule. "I have to go to class with kids I don't even know."

Bridget said brightly, as she wrote notes and directions for each class on her schedule, "At least band is first period, so we can start the day together."

Tommy elbowed Dale. "Look, there's that principal guy we met, and he is heading for the stage. What's his name?" Tommy asked, pointing to the stage.

Bridget abruptly pulled Tommy's arm down. "Don't point! It's not polite. I wrote his name down on my schedule right here. His name is Mr. Hamilton."

Mr. Hamilton walked briskly across the stage to a large wooden podium with a yellow and black banner on the front that read East Libertyville Junior High. He took the mike from the podium and announced in a large, booming voice, "Good morning to our new class of seventh-grade students from Emerson, Wilson, and Jackson elementary schools."

The nervous energy of the students dissipated at the sound of Mr. Hamilton's voice, and the students talking quieted. "I said, *Good Morning*." Mr. Hamilton paused and put his hand to his ear. From a row near the back, P.J. popped up and shouted back, "Good morning." Seeing that he was the only one who answered, he quickly sat down.

Mr. Hamilton laughed and said again, "Good morning," as he gestured for all the students to answer. Finally, the class answered with a thunderous response of "good morning," and there was a round of laughter. Mr. Hamilton gestured for quiet.

"That's more like it. I want to welcome you to one of the finest junior highs in all of Indiana. We have a tradition of excellence that I hope you will embrace and become a part of.

We believe your future successes are in your hands. The staff and faculty are here to challenge you in the classroom, on the athletic field, and in our outstanding music and art programs. Your success here will be because you join a variety of activities and begin to develop into well-rounded young adults. If you look at the banner, you will see our mascot is the lion and our motto is *Roar to Success*. We not only believe the motto, but we also live the motto. Lastly, I would like to have you begin to think of yourselves as the Class of 1951. This will be the year you graduate from high school, which is only six short, exciting years from now."

A low chatter emerged from the audience as the students realized that high school graduation wasn't too far away.

Mr. Hamilton held his hands up once more for quiet and continued, "Today, you will follow the schedule in your packet. You will meet new teachers, make new friends, and become familiar with our school, or should I say, your school. Your classes are fifty minutes long. You will hear a bell that ends each class and then another bell that signals the beginning of the next class. The time between the classes is five minutes and is designed for you to move quickly to your next class. It's not a time to stand and socialize. Remember, today is for seventh graders only. Tomorrow, the eighth graders will join us. Thank you for your attention, and go Lions! When the bell rings, please go to your first period class."

The students began clapping and cheering as Mr. Hamilton left the stage.

"I've never even thought about high school and being called the Class of 1951. I feel so grown up," Chrissy said excitedly.

P.J. looked at his schedule frowning. "I hope I don't get lost and am late to class. Five minutes seems kind of short when you don't know where you are going in a three-story building."

The bell rang and the gang moved out of the auditorium. "At least we know the way to first period band," Dave said, pushing through the crowd of students standing in the hallway looking at their maps.

Mr. Jeffrey greeted them at the door by shaking each student's hand. "Good morning. Please find your name on one of the chairs. That will be the section and seat where you will sit each day until we have chair auditions."

The group split up, scanning the curved rows of chairs and music stands for their names.

Dave shouted, "I found mine. What about you, Dale?"

"Yours is easy since you're a drummer, and you're always in the back."

"No, not a drummer," Dave corrected. "A percussionist." The other seventh-grade percussionists laughed and slapped Dave on the back.

Dale couldn't find his name on the left side of the room and realized that was where the woodwinds sat. He sauntered over to the right side where he found Victor, Karl, and the other brass players already seated.

"Dale, I think you're over here by me." Sandra motioned to him from across the room.

Dale found his name on the second chair in the cornet section. What he saw next made his heart pound. Under his name someone had scrawled

Dale Kingston - Cornet

WELCOME TO MY SECTION!
HOW DOES IT FEEL TO BE SECOND BEST?

Dale stood in front of his chair, staring at the handwritten note, remembering all of his previous confrontations with Jim Petris, the eighth-grade bully and cornet player. His thoughts flashed back to the day of his audition for band. As he climbed the steps of East Libertyville Junior High, Jim had called him a hotshot, blocking him from entering the door. Then Jim disrupted his audition, causing him to mess up his last sight-reading for Mr. Jeffrey.

Other encounters with Jim began rushing into his mind. He remembered how Jim and his friends confronted him on the street outside his house and how Scout defended Dale by chasing Jim up a tree and biting the back pocket off of Jim's jeans. Dale's heart raced as he remembered finding his pumpkins and watermelons smashed in his Victory Garden that he had grown all summer. Dale's stomach turned into knots as he thought of the final confrontation in the park during the celebration for the end of World War II. Jim and his friends cornered Dale in the crowd. He could still hear Jim's threatening voice, "Can't find your friends, big shot? And, I don't see that tough dog here to protect you either." But what made Dale the angriest were Jim's parting words. "Don't worry, Kingston. Your time will come when you come to junior high, and oh ... by the way, how are those pumpkins and watermelons you've been growing?" Those words confirmed that Jim and his friends had been the ones who had destroyed his garden. Dale could feel his anger building, only to have his thoughts interrupted by a voice.

"Dale, can you please take your seat? We are ready to begin." Dale turned toward the voice only to find that he was the only one in the band room not seated. He shook his head to clear his mind and took his seat, still unable to focus on the voice he heard. "Dale, are you all right?"

Dale looked up from his chair to see Mr. Jeffrey staring at him from the podium. All the other students' eyes were focused on him. "Sorry, Mr. Jeffrey," Dale mumbled.

"Let's make sure that doesn't happen again." Mr. Jeffrey turned back to the band, explaining the rehearsal procedures they would follow tomorrow at their first full rehearsal with both the seventh and eighth graders.

Dale tried to concentrate on what Mr. Jeffrey was saying, but he could only think of the handwritten words. "Welcome to my section! How does it feel to be second best?"

Chapter 4

Mission Accomplished

Dale was glad to be walking home alone after saying goodbye to his friends who were going to Victor's house after school. He knew he would miss a lively discussion about everything that had happened during their first day of school. But all that seemed inconsequential compared to his feelings about reading the note on his chair from Jim Petris. Dale wasn't sure how he felt. He was mad, scared, and confused about how to handle tomorrow's rehearsal and facing Jim and his friends. What bothered him the most, however, was he did not understand how to deal with a bully like Jim. Dale had always felt confident in what he did, but now he was unsure. *Is this what junior high is going to be like? Do I need to be tough like Jim?* It was all so confusing. Dale needed this time alone to sort things out. He didn't think his friends would be able to understand what he was going through.

Dale was so deep into thought that he didn't see Scout charging down the street toward him, excited to see his loyal master after being alone all day. Scout leaped full force toward Dale, knocking him to the grass. The dog licked his face, waking Dale from his heavy thoughts.

The boy put his arms around Scout and gave him a big hug and belly scratch. "Thanks for taking my mind off today. I don't think there is anybody I would like to see more than you right now." Dale felt a hand on his shoulder, and a voice he recognized say, "You mean that Scout is more important than I am?"

Dale whipped around to find his father standing behind him. Dale scrambled to his feet and gave his father a hug.

"I'm surprised you didn't see me as you were walking. You must have had some day to be so distracted."

"Never mind my day. When and how did you get home?"

"That's a long story. Pick up your stuff, and I'll tell you all about it." Dale's father put his arm around his son's shoulders. "I want you to know that I'm home for good now that the war is over. We can be a family again."

Scout barked twice as if understanding and took off toward the porch where Dale's mother and grandparents were waiting.

When they got to the porch, Dale's mom greeted him. "Do you remember when your grandfather told you that I left early on a secret mission? My mission was to pick up your dad and bring him home." She put her arms around Dale's dad.

"We wanted it to be a surprise and not take away from your first day as a seventh grader. When we got home, your dad couldn't wait to see you, so he walked up the street to meet you. It looks like you were deep in thought and didn't even see him until Scout knocked you down."

Dale looked down and said, "I guess my first day of junior high kind of filled up my head with stuff, but it's not important now that Dad is home." Then he brightened, "Do I have to wash windows? Could we sit on the porch as a family and talk? What do you say?"

"I heard all about what you did from your mom. I think the punishment can begin tomorrow if everyone agrees," said father, eyeing Grandma carefully. "I do want to hear your side of the bridge and fish story firsthand. Sounds like one heck of a way to finish your list and end your summer."

Grandma headed into the house and said crisply, "OK, tomorrow it is. Let me get some lemonade, and we can sit on the porch and hear about each other's exciting day."

Dale called after her, "Is that a roast I smell cooking?"

"Sure is, and to think it's not even Sunday. Jake, tell us what happened to you once the war ended," Grandpa said as he sat down.

After everyone took a swig of the freshly squeezed lemonade, Dad began. "On August 6th, we were on the island of Okinawa preparing for the invasion of mainland Japan called Operation Downfall when we heard about the first atomic bomb *Little Boy* being dropped. It was followed three days later by another bomb, *Fat Man.* We were really nervous about having to do another invasion because we lost a lot of men during the Okinawa battle. When the Japanese finally surrendered on August 15th, we had to continue to be on alert because not all the Japanese soldiers were aware the war had ended. We were nervous and hoped we wouldn't be one of the last to die while we waited for the final terms of surrender to be signed. As we waited for news of the final signing, our commander explained how soldiers would get to come home. It was called the Advanced Service Rating Score and was based upon the number of points a soldier had earned. You got one point for each month of service, one point for each month overseas, five points for combat awards, and finally twelve points for children under eighteen."

"So I was worth twelve points and helped get you home?"

Dale's dad laughed and tousled his son's hair. "You're worth a lot more than twelve points, but yes, you did help get me home. Once I knew I was coming home, I sent a telegram to your mom that I would be arriving in San Diego on September 3rd."

"That was the same day as my bridge adventure, and also the day the Japanese signed the final surrender agreement on the U.S.S. Missouri."

"I'm really impressed you know about the surrender. How did you learn that?"

"Grandpa read it in the newspaper this morning. My new history teacher, Mr. Battershell, discussed it in class and stressed the importance of understanding history and being well read about current events."

"Sounds like you have a great teacher for your favorite subject. Now let me finish before you tell us more about your day. Lucky for me, your mom was doing one of her last duties as a WASP pilot ferrying troops home. She pulled some strings with General Packston, and I hitched a ride on her plane. She flew us back to Libertyville. She's one great pilot."

Dale looked proudly at his mother. "So are you done flying for the military?"

"Yes, today was my last flight, and I've completed my duty."

"Done, like you won't fly anymore, or done and you will fly but not for the military?"

"I'm not sure what the future is for women in aviation, but during the next several months, we'll find out. For now, I can relax and enjoy having my family back together. We've been separated on and off for four years, and we need to get back to living life without a war to think about."

"I agree. How about we start getting the family back together over dinner? I'm starving."

Dad stood up. "The way you've grown since I've been gone, I can see why you're hungry. Let's eat and hear about your day, Dale. I'm sure you have a lot to tell us." He put his arm around Dale as they went to the dining room table.

The newly united family sat around the table for several hours sharing stories of the summer and Ravinia, riding in a locomotive, learning to shoot skeet, and ending with the final adventure for the summer, fishing from the bridge at Dawson's Lake.

Dad interrupted, "Wait, you jumped off the trestle because a train was coming? Which span of the bridge was it?"

"It was the first one between the shore and the first pylon. We swam there the last time you were home and discussed which part of the lake was the deepest. I remember you saying that before swimming and jumping into water, you have to find out how deep the water is and if there are any obstructions under the water. Remember, we checked the depth of the quarry before putting Tommy's rope swing up so that it was safe. And I remember you telling me that that part of the lake was where the divers from the military base went to practice."

"That explains why you jumped then. You knew it was deep enough," Dad said as he placed his napkin on the table. "I want to warn you that what you did was still risky and dangerous."

Giving Dale's dad a disapproving look, Grandma remarked, "I still think you took too big a risk."

"I agree, but what about your first day at school?"

Dale delayed answering his father by taking a bite of his dessert and gulping it down with some milk.

"Dale, you know what I think about washing your food down without chewing it," Grandma scolded. Then she reconsidered her harshness and said gently, "But tell us about your day. You seem more hesitant to talk than usual."

Dale began slowly with meeting Principal Hamilton and the assembly before band, but he left out the band rehearsal and the note from Jim Petris. He continued to share the names of his teachers and what they taught, adding proudly that each teacher and most of the students knew who he was from the 4th of July jazz concert in the square. When he finished, he sat back and patted his stomach.

"Sounds like you had a good first day. I think this year will be a great one for us to do more together as a family again. How about you and I sit on the porch with some coffee while your grandparents and your mom clean up? I think that after tonight, we aren't going to get out of clean-up chores ... but tonight, let's enjoy.

"All right you two," Grandma said as she popped up to clear the table. "I'll get the coffee and bring it out."

Dale and his dad sat on the porch enjoying the sunset and early evening breeze. "You know, Dale, I've missed doing things with you. I'm looking forward to our time together. But, I'm wondering, you were distracted on the street when you were walking home, and several times tonight you seemed lost in thought. I know I've been away, but I don't ever remember you being so serious or illusive. We have a good relationship, and I want you to feel free to tell me anything that is on your mind. I won't judge you. I'll listen and be there for you."

Dale took a sip of his coffee and began to tell his father everything beginning with the first confrontation with Jim Petris on the steps of the junior high. Dale's dad did not interrupt. Dale finished his story by saying, "I couldn't tell Mom, Grandma, or Grandpa. They would have gotten involved and marched right over to Jim's house and confronted him. I felt I needed to work it out and not overreact. But now, I'm not so sure what to do."

Dad sat still for a few minutes, looking at the final rays of light. "First, I want you to know that you've grown into a fine young man. I know it's hard for you to tell me these things. I understand not wanting to run and tell your mom, which would make you feel like a tattletale. But, talking about this now is important, since it will allow us to work through your feelings. I've faced bullies, too. However, never once did I use physical force. Do you remember what I told you years ago about fighting?"

"I think so. You said, a Kingston never throws the first punch, but we will always defend ourselves, our friends, and especially our family."

"That's right. Fighting is a last resort. Sometimes you have to reach deep inside yourself, decide who you are and what you stand for. I can't, no one can do that for you. But, I can tell you that once you step up to the challenges in life, you will begin the journey into adulthood."

Dale sat thinking about what his dad had said for a few minutes. "Thanks for the support. I feel a lot better about the situation. You won't tell Mom, will you? She'll only worry."

"I won't tell her until the time is right. I promise."

Dale gave his dad a hug. "Can we go for a morning run tomorrow? I've missed working out with you."

"OK, tomorrow we work out. Now come here and shake my hand."

Dale shook his father's strong hand, sealing their bond as father and son. The screen door creaked, signaling Dale's mom had entered the porch. "Time for bed! It's been a long day, and tomorrow is a school day."

As Dale climbed the stairs to his room, he thought, *you have to step up to the challenges in life. If you do, you will begin the journey into adulthood.*

Chapter 5

ADVICE

Dale awoke early to surprise his father by making coffee before their first workout. The strong smell of freshly brewed coffee filled the kitchen when Dale's dad bounded down the stairs in his P.T. ranger t-shirt.

"This is a welcome surprise on my first morning back. It smells great. Did you make that pot of coffee yourself?"

Handing a cup to his father, Dale said, "Sometimes before I exercise, I make myself a pot. Just the smell wakes me up. Then when the rest of the family gets up, they can get a cup right away and not have to wait."

Dad smiled. "I guess you're a true Swede after all. Now let's see how you've improved since I was last home. You take the lead."

Jogging out the back door, Dale took off at a brisk pace with his father in pursuit. After the third run up Simpson Hill, Dale was sweating heavily, but he was still trying to stay ahead of his father. Turning the last corner before reaching home, Dale could hear his father's footsteps getting closer and knew that he would try to pass him, so he picked up the pace. With less than a hundred yards left, Dale began to tire just as his father pulled alongside.

"So you think you can beat the old man, do you? Let's see what you've got left. Loser does the dishes tonight." No answer was needed, and Dale took off with what little strength he had left. They were still neck and neck when Dad surged ahead at the last minute and won by ten feet.

"I'm very impressed with how fast you have gotten. If I'd known you were that fast, I might not have bet you on doing the dishes."

"It was close," Dale gasped while he caught his breath and headed to the garage for the second part of the workout, which consisted of pull-ups, chin-ups, sit-ups, and push-ups. But, when Dale walked into the garage, he saw three old mattresses spread on the ground. "Where did these come from? They weren't here yesterday."

"After our discussion last night on the porch and hearing about Jim Petris, I thought I would teach you a little self-defense. I can give you some suggestions on how to deal with bullies. I've seen bullies as both a kid and an adult, and maybe if I share with you what I learned, it will help you learn to deal with them. But remember, we never start a fight; we only defend ourselves. And we will defend ourselves both physically and mentally. Let's get started."

For the next thirty minutes, Dad showed Dale the fundamentals of self-defense. First, he learned to always be aware of the situation and not put himself in a position where he would be alone, which would be to the bully's advantage. Next, he learned how to use his own body weight and that of an attacker to defend himself. At the very end, Dad had Dale pretend to attack him. Using the techniques he had just shown him, Dad was able to pin Dale to the mat in one simple move.

Dale sat up and leaned back on his elbows. "Am I glad you put those mats down. That would have hurt to land on the ground like I did."

"I hope you can see that by using your weight and this first simple move you can avoid being hurt in a fight. This is only for defense. We will learn a little more each time we work out. In no time, you'll be able to do the same to me."

Dad pulled up a bench. "Now, sit down for a minute. Let's talk about how to deal with bullies and not be intimidated by them. Bullies want to see a reaction from you, but this is what you can do. First, stand tall and be brave if confronted. That way, it looks like you are not intimidated. Next, if possible, ignore them and do not make eye contact. Act as though you don't hear them or see them, which will confuse them. If possible, always try and be with a friend or two. A bully is less likely to confront you if you are with someone. And finally, don't show you are upset, because that is what they want. The more you control your emotions, the more frustrated they become and will back off. There are two kinds of bullies: the physical kind who hit, punch, or destroy things, and the verbal kind who tease, name call, taunt, spread rumors, or gossip about you. This Jim kid sounds like he is a little bit of both, so be ready for physical and verbal bullying. I know that's a lot to remember, but we'll work on self-defense and talk about more strategies now that I'm home."

Dale looked up at his dad in appreciation. "Thanks for helping me feel better about the situation. I promise not to fight and will only use what you teach me as a last resort."

"Excellent! Let's go get some more of that coffee you made. I think I smell bacon and eggs."

Chapter 6

The Rehearsal

By the time Dale and the gang had gotten to school, Dale had caught up on his friends' first-day-of-school experiences. He also shared about his dad coming home and his mom flying her last mission for the Air Force because the WASPs were not needed anymore, since the war was over.

"I sure hope your mom can keep flying. She is a great pilot, and I want her to take me for another plane ride," Sandra added, recalling the fun she had while flying with Mrs. Kingston last summer.

"She said she didn't know what the future is for women in aviation, but I'm sure she'll find work flying somewhere," Dale said as they turned onto the street across from the junior high.

The group came to a sudden stop. P.J. looked in wonder at the crowd in front of the building. "This is twice as crowded as yesterday. I'll bet the halls will be jammed when we go from class to class."

Bridget dismissed P.J.'s comment. "I'm not worried. I found all my classes yesterday and think we'll all do just fine. Let's hurry up and get to band." Bridget grabbed Chrissy's hand. "We don't want to be the last to sit down, plus I want to meet the other eighth-grade saxophone players. I want to hear them warm up and see how good they are. If I'm going to try out for jazz band, I'd better size up the competition." Chrissy nodded and giggled. "And maybe we can meet some cute boys!"

Victor made a gagging sound, and the gang laughed.

By the time they made their way down the hall to the band room, they could hear students warming up. Dale had been scanning the throngs of students looking for Jim Petris and his friends, but so far, he hadn't seen them in the crowd. He began to relax.

Mr. Jeffrey was standing at the door of the band room like the day before, shaking each student's hand. "Welcome to your first rehearsal. I'm really looking forward to hearing what we sound like. Now go inside and sit in the same seat as yesterday. Remember, when I step on the podium, you should be seated and warmed up."

"Mr. Jeffrey, are you going to greet us each morning?" Tommy asked, stepping forward to shake Mr. Jeffrey's hand.

"Absolutely! I think it's important to welcome my students and get a feeling for the day. Some days, junior high students are more wound up than other days, but today you all seem pretty calm. Now warm up and meet your other band mates."

As the group moved into the band room, the atmosphere was completely different from the day before. Students were moving back and forth between the instrument lockers and their chairs, some were chatting excitedly about their summer experiences, others were warming up, and a few were greeting the new seventh-grade band students.

"Welcome to band. My name is Adrianne Pepperage, and I'm the band president and flute section leader." She quickly glanced down at the case in Chrissy's hand. "You must be Chrissy Rule."

"Nice to meet you, but how did you know who I am?"

Adrianne said smugly, "I learned the names and faces of my flute section by getting a copy of each of the elementary school band programs and class pictures. Mr. Jeffrey believes that it's our job as section leaders to lead by example. I want you to know that I care about each person in the section and will do anything I can to help you." She turned and ushered Chrissy to her chair in the circle in front of the podium.

"I came to your last concert with some other ELJH band students when you played that awesome flute solo from memory." Before Chrissy could answer, Adrianne turned and returned to the rest of the gang, calling them by name and giving them a quick handshake.

When she got to Dale, her voice and manner changed. "Hi," she cooed and extended her hand. "You must be Dale Kingston. I've wanted to meet you ever since I saw you in the square receiving that engraved cornet from Mr. Greenleaf. But you look so much taller and stronger up close," she said, slowly releasing Dale's hand. "I hope you'll run for a band office so we can work together."

Dale blushed, stunned by Adrianne's warm, inviting voice and sparkling brown eyes. Dale was saved when P.J. stepped up to Adrianne, holding out his hand.

"I'm P.J. Walsh, the other young man who helped save the town."

Adrianne, annoyed at the intrusion, smirked. "Oh, that's right. You're the one who rode down the street in your pajamas."

P.J. looked wounded. "Do you think I look taller and stronger, too?" he asked hopefully.

"No, about the same," Adrianne said brushing him aside, but not before giving Dale a slight smile.

P.J. and Dale stood in awe as Adrianne floated through the crowd to greet another group of students. Sandra jostled them back to reality. "Put your eyes back in your heads and go warm up, Mr. Taller and Stronger," she said, causing them to laugh as they got their horns out of their cases. As Dale stood, he heard a familiar but not welcome voice behind his back.

"Hey, hotshot. Looks like you finally get to hear what a real trumpet sounds like." Putting the trumpet to his lips, Jim played several two-octave scales that went up to high C and D.

Dale remembered what his dad had said and just turned, being sure not to make eye contact or react to his words or playing. Keeping his eyes to the front of the room, Dale crossed the room, sat down, and began to play his long tones and arpeggios. Playing made him feel better and helped to take his attention away from Jim.

Most of the students were seated when Jim slipped into his seat as first chair and whispered menacingly, "You didn't get the folder like you were supposed to. Go down to the rack in the front of the room and get folder forty-six. That's our folder, and second chair players always get the music for rehearsal." Dale turned to look into Jim's cold black eyes. Without saying anything, he got up to get the folder. As he returned to his seat, he realized he was the only student not in his seat. Mr. Jeffrey stood on the podium and tapped his baton. Dale froze.

"Dale, why aren't you seated like the rest of the band? You know my rule about being ready in your seat before I step on the podium. Now, get back to your seat so we can begin."

Dale started to answer, but he realized that he had been tricked. Anything he said would just add to his embarrassment. He set the folder firmly on the stand, getting out the chorale book and turning to the page Mr. Jeffrey had written on the board. As Mr. Jeffrey raised his baton, Jim leaned in close so no one could hear and whispered, "Gotcha."

Dale just put his horn up to his lips and waited for Mr. Jeffrey to begin. It seemed forever before he gave the downbeat, but when it finally came, Dale felt relieved to play. He focused on the rehearsal, briefly taking his mind off of Jim and getting in trouble.

The band sounded good, especially since they were sight-reading. Mr. Jeffrey would stop the band and make corrections as they played. Several times, Jim made simple playing mistakes, which Mr. Jeffrey corrected by addressing the trumpet section. Each time Mr. Jeffrey stopped, Jim would turn and look despairingly at Dale, as if Dale had made the error. Dale, who was a good sight-reader, was annoyed, but now wasn't the time to draw attention to Jim's mistakes.

At the end of rehearsal, Mr. Jeffrey announced that he wanted to see the brass quintet of Dale, Victor, Sandra, P.J., and Karl at the podium before they put their horns away. Then he thanked the band for a good first rehearsal and reminded them that auditions for chairs would be in eight weeks, after the seventh graders got used to junior high. Audition music was on the table in the front of the room. Once the band was dismissed, Dale got up quickly and moved down to the podium where Mr. Jeffrey was waiting. In a loud voice, he heard, "Hey, Kingston! Don't forget to put the folder away," followed by laughter from Jim's friends.

Mr. Jeffrey looked up from the podium. "Excuse me, Jim. Did you say that it was Dale's job to put the folder away? I don't think so," and he stepped off the podium, and approached Jim. "First, I don't like your tone of voice to a fellow band member, and I especially don't think it's fair for

Dale to put it away since he had to get it before rehearsal. As section leader, you should have done that the first day. So, I think you'll put the folder away. And, I don't want any more examples of you not leading your section. Section leader is not a given; it's earned," he said, giving Jim a stern look.

Turning back to Dale, Mr. Jeffrey said, "It looks like you had an interesting first day of band. I hope we don't have any rivalry going on between the two of you. We're all working for the same goal, and that is to be the best band we can. That's why I wanted to talk to you five." Mr. Jeffrey's voice softened as he explained how he wanted the original brass quintet to stay together and perfect their skills before contest in the spring.

"If it's OK with you, I'd like to rehearse with you one morning each week. If we start now, we can take our time developing the skills you'll need to compete."

"Why us, when you have so many great eighth-grade players?" Karl said.

"I do have some great older players, but you have chemistry between you that I don't see in groups very often. I want to foster it and see how far we can go musically. What do you say?"

The group looked at each other and agreed it would be fun to keep the ensemble together. Maybe they could get some more church jobs and save some money for another trip such as the one they took to Ravinia.

"Great! You'll practice Thursday mornings beginning this week at 7:15, which will give us a good half hour before the band arrives for rehearsal. See you tomorrow."

The group moved to the instrument storage room lockers to put their horns away. Dale was just putting his horn in his locker when the bell rang. He hurriedly slammed the locker door, and turned to face Jim and two of his friends. Remembering what his father had advised, Dale took a deep breath, stood tall, and squared his shoulders. He decided to speak first to disrupt whatever Jim's plan was.

"Great rehearsal today, Jim. Oh...hi Adrianne," Dale added, causing Jim and his friends to turn. Dale then slipped past Jim and his friends, making as little physical contact as possible.

"Hi, Dale," Adrianne replied. "Where's your next class?"

Before answering, Dale turned back and looked square into Jim's eyes. He whispered, "Gotcha!" Then as he ushered Adrianne out of the locker room, he said, "English. What's yours?

Jim hissed, "Nice move, Kingston, but this is just your first day. I won't make it so easy for you next time."

Once in the hallway, Adrianne said, "What did Jim say to you?"

"Nothing, I think he was saying something about him getting the folder tomorrow."

Adrianne laughed. "After the chewing out he got today from Mr. Jeffrey, I'm sure he won't do that again." Her hand gently brushed his as they parted to go to second period.

Chapter 7

REPRIEVE

Saturday dawned cool and breezy, with just a few clouds dotting the horizon. Dale had finished a leisurely run with Scout by his side. As he crossed the yard back to his house, he reviewed his first week at school. Minus a few confrontations with Jim, the week had gone fairly well. He had made so many new friends that he was rarely alone in the halls, which helped keep Jim at a distance for now. He liked his classes, but the homework was harder than in elementary school. The brass quintet had a good first rehearsal, and today, he finally ended his week-long punishment for jumping off the trestle.

His father couldn't exercise this morning, since he had been asked to return to the railroad as an engineer on one of the new diesel locomotives that were replacing the old steam engines. He'd been assigned to the passenger line, the *Pioneer Zephyr,* nicknamed "The Silver Streak" because of the low-profile front engine and stainless steel outside that shined brightly in the sun. Dale accompanied his father to the station to admire the beautiful engine and train. He hoped to get a ride on it to Chicago someday, although he thought it couldn't top his ride on the steam engine with his grandfather last summer.

After finishing his run, he opened the back door to the kitchen and his stomach let out a loud growl, causing his mother and grandparents to look up.

"I guess from the sound of your stomach you need some food. Sit down," Grandma said as she heaped eggs, fresh bacon, and toast onto a plate for Dale.

"Great pot of coffee, Dale. Thanks for having it ready for us," said Mother as he sat down. "Are you glad your punishment is over today?"

Dale nodded as he pushed his eggs onto the fork with his toast. "I think I learned my lesson. I had some time to think about how foolish my jumping off the trestle was. It won't happen again, I promise. But, the best part of being done is that I can go over to Mr. Edwards with the gang and listen to some of his recordings of great jazz musicians. When we were on the train to Chicago this summer, he invited us over. I can't wait to hear some great jazz trumpet players. It'll get me ready for the jazz band tryouts in two weeks."

"Well, they say if you can't hear it, you can't play it. The more you listen, the better you get," Grandpa said.

Dale thought about what Grandpa said. "I think I have gotten better from listening to jazz. May I be excused? I'm sure the gang will be coming early to pick me up to ride to Mr. Edwards's house. We also want to go swimming in the quarry one last time before it gets too cold. We're ready to blow off some steam after a whole week of school."

"Yes, you may be excused. Say hello to Mr. Edwards from me. Tell him I miss his good ole Louisiana cooking!" Grandpa said.

"Sure will!" Dale put his dishes in the sink to prepare for his friends' arrival.

Chapter 8

Letting Off Steam

Bridget was the last one out of the water, joining the rest of the gang lying on the cool granite stones of the quarry in the warm afternoon sun. "I don't think I'll ever get enough of your rope swing, Tommy. It sure is nice of you guys to let us join you."

"Wait, they aren't letting us," Chrissy said as she flipped over to warm her back. "Remember, we won the bet fair and square when we beat them at Capture the Flag."

Victor joined in. "Either way, what a day! I needed that bike race, which I won, of course. And, listening to records with Mr. Edwards was cool. But the greatest part is being able to swim here with my best friends."

"Wow, that's so sentimental of you, Victor. If you don't stop, I'm going to cry," Sandra said as she squeezed the water from her long ponytail.

"I know we're seventh graders, but it's still fun to do the same things we did as a group back in elementary school," Dave replied.

"What do you mean when we were back in elementary school? You make it seem like it's been years when it's only been three months," said Bridget.

Dale admitted, "With all that has happened over the summer and this first week of school, it seems like years."

P.J. leaned over onto his elbows. "By the way, what's the deal with you, Jim Petris, and that Adrianne girl? She really gave you a look and gave me a dirty look."

"I don't know about her, but Jim ..." Dale paused before he added, "Can I tell you something in secret?"

They all sat up and looked at Dale. "What do you mean secret? Like we can't tell anybody kind of secret?" Bobby said.

Dale nodded. "Exactly ... we can talk to each other, but no one outside of the gang needs to know. I'm not going to tell you about this if you all don't swear to keep it between us. Now swear!" And in unison they all recited, "Cross my heart and hope to die, stick a needle in my eye."

All eyes were on Dale as he related his run-ins with Jim and his friends. He left out the part about his Dad teaching him self-defense, but he ended with the story about how he'd been tricked by Jim into getting the folder, and the resulting confrontation at the band lockers and making a quick get-away using Adrianne. When he finished, they sat in silence until Chrissy spoke up. "I knew something was wrong when you were so quiet. I saw Jim say something to you in rehearsal right before you got up. I saw the whole thing because I sit right across from you. But what I don't get is why you couldn't tell us? That is one of the first rules when dealing with a bully. You must tell your friends who can support you and look out for you." Chrissy hesitated before continuing. "Speaking for Bridget and Sandra, we have a confession to make also. Does everyone still want to keep this conversation between us and no one else?"

The gang moved closer together and agreed to keep it between themselves.

Chrissy took a deep breath. "OK, I think we'll feel a lot better if we get this out in the open. Sandra, do you want to tell the story?"

Sandra cleared her throat and began. "We shouldn't get after Dale for not telling us about Jim because we haven't been exactly open about some of our encounters with Jim and his friends. A few weeks after we dunked him in the dunk tank at the Fourth of July celebration, the three of us were walking back from the library. We were talking and laughing and not paying attention to our surroundings when Jim and three of his friends cornered us in the empty lot right behind your house, Dale. I don't know what they were doing there, but they caught us alone. Jim did most of the talking, but the other boys surrounded us, and we were scared. Jim started taunting us about being alone, and maybe we aren't so tough like we were at the dunk tank. He got in Bridget's face and talked tough, and we didn't know what to say. We were so shocked. Finally, I kind of lost it and stepped up into his face and shouted at him. "So you think you're a tough kid by picking on girls? I don't think you and your friends are so tough." And I pushed him away from Bridget. Well, Scout must have heard me, and he came flying through the grass, barking and growling something fierce. He got between us and the boys—bared his teeth and snapped at them. You should have seen them take off. After you told us how Scout had treed Jim and his friends, and tore Jim's pocket off his jeans, I can see why they took off. Scout chased them for a little bit, but we called him back."

Chrissy added, "I love your dog, Dale. He saved us, but we couldn't tell you. We were afraid you would go after Jim and defend us. We're sorry for not saying anything. Can you forgive us?"

Dale got up and hugged each of the girls. "You were so brave. Sandra, I'm so proud of you for standing up for Bridget. I think you were right in not telling us, but now that we know, let's remember to share and protect each other."

"Just like the Three Musketeers! All for one, and one for all!" Bobby shouted, raising his hand in the air like the Musketeers.

"If Jim and his friends mess with me, I'll punch him," Victor vowed.

Dale shook his head. "No, that's not how to deal with a bully. That's the last resort. I want everyone to promise we will defend ourselves, but not throw the first punch. We can deal with them in other ways."

The friends discussed how they would handle the different situations until Tommy finally said, "Enough of dumb old Jim and his friends. Let's swim." He jumped up and grabbed the rope swing and glided out over the quarry before letting go and shouting, "All for one, and one for all!" right before hitting the water. The rest of the afternoon was spent swimming and enjoying the warm September sun. The gang was relieved that they had opened up to each other about Jim. When the Conn Factory five o'clock whistle blew, they packed up their backpacks and headed home, dropping each friend off until only Chrissy and Dale were riding up Simpson Hill as they had done together so many times.

"Chrissy, when you're done with dinner, come over and sit with me and my family on the porch. Let's watch the sunset together."

"I'd love to. I can't think of anyone else other than Scout I would rather do that with," she said as they parted ways and headed home.

Chapter 9

CONFESSION

It had been four weeks since the gang had opened up to each other at the quarry, and school was in full swing. The band members were preparing for chair tryouts, and tension was running high. Each student understood the importance of this audition, since there wouldn't be another one until March. The seventh graders wanted to prove they had improved, and the eighth graders were trying to keep the chairs and leadership positions they had earned at the end of seventh grade. Jim and his friends knew something had changed because the gang always made a point of being in groups and not letting Jim and his friends catch them alone.

Dale continued to exercise in the morning with his father when he was home. If he worked out alone, then Scout was his trusted companion, watching his back. Dale was getting much better at learning how to defend himself and talked often to his dad about ways to handle various situations with a bully. But this Friday morning in October was special. Dad had told Dale that today was the day he had to reverse positions with him. Now Dad would be the attacker, and Dale would be the defender.

As usual, Dale was up early making the coffee and thinking through all the moves he had learned.

"Morning," Dad said, entering the kitchen and pouring a quick cup of coffee. "I say this morning we do a short run and then let's see what you can do. You're definitely ready to show me what you've learned."

"I'm a little nervous, but I'll try my best."

"You'll do fine," Dad said as they headed out the back door. "Only one time up and down the hill. That will warm us up."

"Sounds good to me," Dale said, keeping up with his father during the run. As they turned the corner to return home, Dale sprinted ahead to win.

"Not fair," Dad complained. "This is supposed to be a warm-up lap."

Dale teased back, "What do you always say to me? All is fair in love and war?"

"You got me on that one," Dad admitted. "Let's get started." First, they reviewed all of the moves Dale had learned and then did some slow-motion practice. "Let's speed some of the moves up. Don't think about what to do ... just let your intuition and muscle memory do the work. Ready?" And, before Dale could answer, his father came straight at him, trying to grab his arms. Without thinking, Dale ducked right, grabbed his father's wrist and stuck his foot out. Then he drove his shoulder into his father's chest, sending him flying over Dale and landing on his back. Dale finished the move by grabbing and twisting his father's wrist backwards and putting his foot on his dad's chest.

"Ouch, these mattresses are not as thick as I thought."

"OK, say uncle, and I'll let you up," Dale said triumphantly, but his dad did not answer. Instead he swung his leg up and over Dale's head, pulling him to the ground and quickly pinning Dale.

"Now you say uncle," his father said with a smile on his face. "You should have made sure you had me securely pinned before calling uncle. Don't think that whoever attacks you will give up. You have to make sure you keep them from getting out of your hold and trying to hurt you. Finish the move." Dad kept the pressure on Dale's chest. "Now you say uncle."

"Uncle, uncle," Dale gasped and Dad released him and helped him up.

"You did great, Dale, for the first time, but I think you learned that it's not over until it's over. Being defensive will help you stay safe, but remember, you must not let your guard down until help comes from an adult or your friends."

"I'll remember ... let's try again."

For the next thirty minutes they practiced different moves, depending on how the attacker made his move. On the last move, Dale was able to toss his father and hold him down until he called for uncle.

As Dale helped his father up, he noticed his mother standing in the garage door, her hand on her hips and a frown on her face.

"What is going on with all these filthy mattresses and Dale tossing you in the air and calling uncle? You know I don't like rough housing and fighting. What's this about?"

Dale and his father looked at each other and his dad sheepishly replied, "Remember when I said I wouldn't tell your mother until it was time? Well, I think it's time."

"Time for what? What is this about, Dale?"

"OK, I'll only tell you if you promise not to get mad or overreact. I want to tell you sitting down inside over coffee. Then, I'll tell you everything."

Mother shook her head. "I'm not going to promise I won't get mad, and I don't like the tone of your voice saying that I might overreact."

Dad stepped in and took Mother by the arm. "Let's calm down and all talk this out," he said as he led her to the house.

Once Mother was seated at the kitchen table next to Grandma and Grandpa, Dad began by explaining that he had asked Dale why he was so distracted the first night he was home. He explained that Dale told him about a run-in with some older boys and how he wanted Dale to learn how to defend himself both physically and verbally. Before letting Dale speak, he added.

"Dale is growing into a fine young man. I think the way he has handled this issue and how we are dealing with it at this time is allowing Dale to try and solve the problem first before we get involved. Now enough from me … Dale, tell your side."

Dale told the story from the beginning while everyone sat quietly. He told about the confrontation on the steps of the junior high and ended with the threat in the band instrument room.

"I know I could've told you before, but I wasn't sure what to do. I wanted to see if I could handle it myself. I know there are different ways of dealing with it, but I chose to try this way first. I wasn't lying to you or anything … I just wasn't sure how to involve other people until Dad came home. Then I felt I could start by telling him. I'm sorry if I've disappointed you."

No one spoke right way and, for Dale, the silence was unbearable. He could see they were thinking about what they both had shared. Finally, Mother leaned forward and said, "First, I'm proud of you for finally sharing. Your grandparents and I had noticed that you seem distracted, and with the garden being smashed, we thought something was going on. I agree with your father that you shouldn't fight first and only defend yourself, although I don't like it. But I've been bullied just as you have, especially being a woman pilot in the military. In the coming weeks, we can have some honest discussions about how I've handled those situations and maybe you'll learn from all of us sharing our experiences. Now give me a hug, and then let's get some food in you before school."

Dale gave his mother and grandmother a hug and shook hands with both his dad and grandfather.

Grandpa patted Dale on the back. "Did you really toss your dad to the floor and force him to call uncle?"

Grandma interrupted, "Enough of the fight talk, C.H. Dale needs to get off to school."

Chapter 10

Lessons Learned

Two weeks had passed since Dale told his mom and grandparents about Jim Petris. Having gotten that burden off his chest, he returned to being his usual lighthearted self with his friends and new classmates. In band rehearsal, Dale listened as Mr. Jeffrey explained the audition procedures, which would take place next week.

"Today is the last rehearsal for the week. Be sure to take your instruments home after school for the weekend, and prepare for your auditions for chair assignments, which begin on Monday. If you've done your work, you'll be fine. If you've procrastinated and not been working each week on your music, then you're about to learn a valuable lesson. And that lesson is that you can't hide or fake a lack of hard work. Let's end today's rehearsal with Pascual Chovi's *Pepita Greus*, which will be one of the audition pieces in addition to the etudes and scales I gave you six weeks ago."

Dale liked the *Pepita Greus,* which started out with a short trumpet solo and reminded him of a bugle call. He wasn't nervous about the audition, since he was second chair and had nothing to lose.

"Dale, I'd like you to play the opening solo since Jim has had his chance. It's time to see what the other members of the section can do. Remember, I don't care what chair you are sitting in. The player who plays it the best will play the solo on the concert."

Dale was suddenly jolted into reality by Mr. Jeffrey's words. "Excuse me, did you say you want me to play the solo instead of Jim?"

Mr. Jeffrey nodded. "Unless you have a problem with that. Do you?"

Dale hesitated, before he regrouped and said, "I'm ready when you are." Dale was afraid to look over at Jim, who he sensed was staring at him. His heart started to pound, his mouth went dry, and he felt flushed all at once when he heard his father's voice remind him: "*Take a deep breath, stand tall, and don't show you're afraid.*"

"Let's start at the beginning and play to letter A. Then we'll repeat that section so that each of the first trumpets can try the solo."

Dale felt as if the world were in slow motion. He saw Mr. Jeffrey raise his baton to give the downbeat, and at the same time, he could see all of his friends and the other band members looking at him. In his mind, he could hear the words, *Take a deep breath, stand tall, and don't show you're afraid.* Down went the baton, and the next thing he saw was Mr. Jeffrey giving the cut-off for the band to stop. Dale shook his head wondering what had just happened. Mr. Jeffrey stood on the podium, looking at him with his mouth wide open.

"What and who in the world was that?" Mr. Jeffrey said.

"What was what?" Dale replied, not knowing what he had played or what had happened.

"That was fantastic! I've never heard you play like that before." Mr. Jeffrey glanced at Jim. "I guess we have ourselves a little friendly competition. Now, let's have the next player, Phil, take a turn."

As Phil prepared to play, Jim moved closer and whispered, "Friendly competition? I don't think so, Kingston. Watch your back."

Dale turned to face Jim's cold black eyes and smiled back, remembering his mother's advice to "*Kill them with kindness.*"

When the rehearsal ended, Dale evaded Jim, who was talking to his friends and gesturing toward Dale's chair. He was relieved when the bell rang so he could go to his next class, English. Then he headed off to gym with Mr. Cabutti whom he liked. For the first six weeks, they played softball, and now they were into their second week of basketball. Dale liked basketball and was looking forward to some exercise to take his mind off band and the upcoming audition.

Mr. Cabutti met Dale and his friends at the locker room door. "I think today I'll have my seventh graders play Mr. Dunkin's eighth graders and get a little friendly competition going between the two." Dale grimaced at the words friendly competition. "I'm getting ready for basketball tryouts soon and would like to see what kind of talent we have." Victor spoke up first: "We're going to smash those eighth graders, if I have anything to say about it."

Dale pulled Victor into the locker room before Mr. Cabutti could answer. "Come on, Victor, lighten up. Save your energy for the game. And do you believe that is the second time I've heard someone say 'friendly competition'?"

Victor admitted he got carried away. "Is it really possible to have a friendly competition?"

"I don't know, but we will find out in a few minutes."

The boys changed into their gym clothes and were standing on the lines of the gym floor for roll call. After they finished the daily calisthenics, the seventh graders filed into the adjoining eighth-grade gym. Dale scanned the eighth-grade class they would play, and what he saw made him swallow hard. There in the group of boys were three of Jim's friends, Pete, Mike, and Joe. They pointed at him and started laughing.

Mr. Dunkin stepped forward. "Looks like you have some good-looking talent, Mr. Cabutti. This should be interesting. Let's play five-on-five full court with a different group of five for the first three quarters. Then the teams with the most points will play against each other the last quarter."

"Sounds fair, Dunkin; give me a minute to divide my class into teams." Mr. Cabutti selected each group of five, spreading out the talent. Dale's team included Victor along with three new kids from Wilson named Fritz, Chuck, and Steve. Dale had played with them earlier in the week. They were really good, and they complemented each other's weaknesses. After the teams were picked, Dale was relieved to see that his team would play the first quarter, while Jim's three friends would play in the second quarter.

"Remember what you've learned in class. Move the ball around, and pass the ball at least four times before shooting. Everybody got it?" Mr. Cabutti held the ball above center court for the initial jump. He blew the whistle and tossed the ball in the air.

During the first quarter, Dale's seventh-grade team scored 20 points and the eighth graders scored 9. In the second quarter, the eighth graders with Jim's friends outscored the seventh graders 22 to 10. The third quarter was even, with both teams scoring 16 points.

"Looks like we have ourselves a game here, Mr. Cabutti." The scoreboard read eighth grade 47, seventh grade 46. "The top scorers will now play each other for the final quarter. Looks like first-quarter seventh graders will play against the second-quarter eighth graders."

Dale shifted from one foot to another as he looked across the court at Jim's friends. He leaned into the huddle as Mr. Cabutti talked strategy. "These guys are fast and rough. You'll need to play great defense and play physically. They're going to bring it to you, hoping you'll back down. Don't rush your play. 'Pass, pass, pass.' Now let's show them what seventh graders can do."

Mr. Dunkin said, "Put ten minutes on the clock, and let's play."

Dale and his team talked about passing as they took their positions on the floor. Victor would do the jump ball. Mike, Jim's friend, inched up next to Dale.

"Looks like I'm guarding you. It's time for some payback, Kingston. I don't see your dog and only one of your friends is here. Time to go down!"

Dale didn't answer, but at the sound of the whistle to start the jump ball, Mike shoved an elbow into Dale's chest sending him to the floor, stunned.

"Come on, Kingston, get in the game!" Mr. Cabutti shouted as the eighth grade scored an easy lay-up while Dale got up.

Dale helped get the ball inbounds to the taunts of Jim's friends. Mike was guarding him close. "So you want some payback?" Dale said right before driving into Mike with his shoulder, sending the eighth grader backwards to the floor and allowing Dale to score an easy lay-up.

On the next eighth-grade inbound pass, Victor intercepted and scored another lay-up, announcing to Mike and Pete, "Is that all you got?"

For the next nine and a half minutes, numerous fouls were called, but more often than not, no fouls were called, which allowed both sides to play a rough, physical game. With thirty seconds left and holding the ball with the scored tied, Mr. Cabutti called for a time-out.

"What a game! We've got the ball, so I want you to stall and cause them to foul you or pass it back and forth until you can get a lay-up. Watch out if you get the lay-up because they'll come and put a big hit on you. I know Mr. Dunkin's coaching style. Stay aware of your surroundings and keep track of where each player is, especially you, Dale. I think those three kids have it out for you."

The team walked onto the floor to the yells and cheers of their fellow students.

Mike was guarding Dale as the ball came inbounds to Dale, but he passed it off before Mike could foul him. The seventh graders passed and dribbled the ball down the court, taking twenty-five seconds off the clock with no opening to be found. Victor took a pass from Steve and dribbled left, away from the basket. Mike, who was guarding Dale, lunged toward Victor to get a jump ball, with his friends Pete and Joe trying to grab the ball. That gave Dale an open lane to the basket if Victor could only get loose.

The three converged on Victor, and with elbows out, Victor was able to fend off the three and pass to Dale who was headed for the basket. Victor's perfect bounce pass caught Dale in full stride as he scooped up the ball and continued to drive to the basket without losing any speed. Dale remembered Mr. Cabutti's comments, *Watch out if you get the lay-up. They'll try and put a big hit on you. Stay aware of your surroundings and keep track of where each player is, especially you, Dale. I think those three kids have it out for you.*

Dale's intuitions came alive as he realized that the three were headed right for him. Anticipating a collision, Dale spun to the right, away from Mike and into Pete's path before jumping out of the way, causing the two eighth graders to collide and fall to the floor in pain. Dale laid the ball in the basket, breaking the tie and winning the game for the seventh graders. His classmates stormed the floor while the two older boys picked themselves up, surprised by Dale's final move.

"Great pass, Victor, and an even better lay-up, Dale!" Mr. Cabutti shouted over the cheering seventh graders.

The two teams made a line and began shaking hands. When Dale got to Mike, Pete, and Joe's hands, he hesitated, not knowing what to expect. Mike put his hand out first. "Great move, Kingston. And, your friend Victor sure is strong. I hope you two think about trying out for the team this year. With moves like that, we could sure use you. See you tomorrow in band."

Dale walked off the court in a daze. "Maybe they realize we're not so bad after all. What do you think, Vic?"

"I don't know. But I do know that was one heck of a game and pass." As they entered the locker room, Dale confided to his friend, "I hope we're done with the friendly competitions for the day. I've had enough excitement."

his friend. "I hope we're done with the friendly competitions for the day. I've had enough excitement."

Chapter 11
THREE LESSONS

Lesson 1

Dale leaned his face toward the car window so he could enjoy the breeze as his father sped down the country road. Scout had his head out the back window sniffing the air that ruffled his ears and fur. They both were in their element today as they drove to the Libertyville Sportsmen's Club.

The night before, while Dale was sharing the events of the day and how he had applied what his parents had told him about dealing with bullies, the phone had rung. The call was for Dale. Dale rarely got phone calls, but this one was special. Mr. Schilke, the first-chair trumpet player with the Chicago Symphony, whom Dale had met on the summer trip to Ravinia, was calling.

Mr. Schilke invited Dale to meet him at the club, where he was competing in a pistol competition. When Dale asked for his signature on the program from the Ravinia concert, Mr. Schilke had heard about Dale from his buddies at the Sportsmen's Club. They had told him about a young boy whose bugle playing saved the Conn instrument factory from burning down. Mr. Schilke, who was an avid marksman, mentioned that if he returned to Libertyville for a pistol competition, perhaps they could shoot together and have a trumpet lesson all in the same day. Dale still couldn't believe that this well-known musician had offered to give him two lessons in one day.

"So, tell me about how Mr. Rule taught you and Chrissy to shoot skeet? I wish I could've taught you, but at least you learned from one of the best. Vern and I have hunted and shot skeet together since we were in grade school."

"Who is Vern?"

"Sorry, Mr. Rule."

"I should have known that, but I have always called him Mr. Rule."

"Until you are older, keep calling him Mr. Rule. That's a sign of respect. I'm sure he'll ask you to start calling him by his first name when you are older."

"How old were you when you learned to shoot?"

"Probably about your age, maybe a year younger. I learned on an old Eastern Arms single shot 410. My father said if you can't hit it in one shot, you have no business hunting with me. I remember that to this day, and that is how you will learn."

"Mr. Rule said the same thing, and that is the kind of shotgun we used."

"Tell me what you learned so I have an idea what you know before we shoot some skeet. I wanted to come out early before meeting Mr. Schilke to spend some time with you and shoot together. If you are good enough, maybe we can go on your first hunt this Thanksgiving for some rabbits or, if we are lucky, some pheasants. What do you think?"

For the remainder of the drive, Dale told his father how Mr. Rule had taught them gun safety and the rules for handling a firearm. They discussed the point that rules were always followed, and if they made a mistake, he would end their training until they were older and more responsible.

"Sounds like he did a thorough job. How'd you do shooting skeet?"

"At first I missed a bunch, but once I got used to leading the skeet, I got pretty good. And you should see Chrissy shoot. Her dad said she was a natural. I don't want to admit it, but she outshot me two out of three times."

"With a little help from me, we should have you ready to take her on next time."

The car wheeled into the dusty parking area. Dad got out of the car. "Let me sign us in, and then we'll drive down to the skeet range before going to the pistol range to meet Mr. Schilke."

Dale felt comfortable at the Sportsmen's Club, since he had been coming here to watch his father shoot before he went to war. It was a short drive to the skeet range that had eight hand-activated skeet throwing machines lined up forty yards apart. The ground in front of the machines was littered with broken orange and black skeet that were made of clay.

"Let's get started. Tell me about the rules as we unload the car."

As they unloaded the car, Dale recited the first four rules of gun safety.

Treat every firearm as if it were loaded.

Always point the muzzle in a safe direction; never point a firearm at anyone or anything you don't want to shoot.

Keep your finger off the trigger and outside the trigger guard until you are ready to shoot.

Keep the action open and the gun unloaded until you are ready to use it.

When he finished those, he continued to list the other eight rules he had learned.

"Excellent! Now, I want you to get the shotgun in that case and show me firsthand how you'll make sure it's unloaded and put it in the rack while I watch."

"Whose gun is this?" Dale asked as he unzipped the soft carrying case.

"It used to be mine"

"What do you mean used to be?"

"It was the one I learned on, and now it's yours to use. I can't think of a better shotgun to start on than one that has been in the family."

For the next hour, they reviewed the rules. Dale's father gave him pointers on how to improve his accuracy as they took turns shooting the skeet that shattered on impact. Dale didn't hear the car pull up as they shot, but when he had finished the round and took out his ear protection, a familiar voice said, "I knew that was you when I drove by. You're a great shot."

Dale set the shotgun safely into the gun rack before shaking Mr. Schilke's hand. "Let me introduce you to my dad."

"Nice to meet you, Mr. Schilke. I've heard a lot about you."

"Thanks for allowing Dale to join me today. And please, call me Renold."

"I think we're all done here, so let's pack up, and we'll meet you up at the pistol range and watch you shoot."

"Before my match, the club is hosting a youth shoot. I'd like Dale to be my guest."

Dad agreed. "I think Dale understands the safety rules enough to be with you. Since my training with pistols was from the military and yours is competitive shooting, it'll be interesting to see the difference between the two."

Dale and his father packed up the guns and leftover skeet and drove to the pistol side of the club. Dale found Mr. Schilke standing with a group of other men near the shooting range.

Lesson 2

"Let's get started. Follow me to the shooting line over here. They haven't announced the range is open, so we have to keep the pistols on the table with the actions open and stand behind this line. Once they announce the range is open, we can pick up the pistols and begin. First, I want to remind you that safety is everything. Guns are not dangerous. People are dangerous. So when you have people and guns together, rules are always followed and never deviated from. Is that understood?"

"Yes, sir."

"One of the first things I want to teach you is how to control your breathing and emotions, and how to stand when shooting. It's very similar to playing an instrument, where you must sit or stand correctly while controlling your emotions and breathing in order to play well. Both are disciplines that require lots of concentration and being able to perform the same skill over and over with great accuracy. Do you understand?"

"I think so."

"Good! Let's put in our earplugs. Protecting your ears when shooting is vital. As a musician, your ears are everything."

Dale and Mr. Schilke put their ear protection in just in time to hear the range office announce that the range was open, meaning they could begin to shoot, and that the range was hot.

Dale walked to the shooting table and the lesson began. Mr. Schilke demonstrated how to stand, hold, pull the trigger, and aim the pistol. After watching him shoot, Dale was ready to give it a try.

"How come the target seems so close?"

"For pistols, this is not close. Since this is a youth shoot, they want you to learn the basics and hit the target. You will see me shoot farther later today."

Dale listened to the final instructions before shooting the pistol for the first time. Since they were shooting single-shot competition pistols, Mr. Schilke would give Dale suggestions and pointers after each shot. It didn't take long for Dale to perfect his shooting technique with the advice from his mentor. Eventually, the range officer announced the range was closed. All guns should be unloaded with the actions open, and everyone should step back from the line. Once that was finished, the range officer walked down the line to check each pistol, confirming they were unloaded and the actions were open before giving the all clear. Taking their earplugs out, Dale walked down range with Mr. Schilke to pick up their targets.

"That sure was fun. I can't believe all that I learned in band applied to shooting."

Mr. Schilke examined the tight ring of holes surrounding the bulls-eye on Dale's targets. "You listened well and obviously you've listened to your music teachers. I'll show you how they score each shot so you know your score. If you understand the scoring system, it will make watching today's competition very exciting."

The rest of the afternoon, Dale and his father sat in the stands watching the competition. They brought binoculars so they could see how each shooter was doing. At the end of each round, the judges would score the targets, announce the scores, and the winners would advance to the next round. At the end of six rounds, the final two shooters were Mr. Schilke and Mr. Garrett, a local sports enthusiast. Watching the two men interact before the final round was fascinating to Dale. They shook hands before the round started, but after that, it was almost as if each one was in his own world. They didn't react to the cheering crowd or the sounds of gunfire coming from other ranges. But what was most impressive to Dale was their posture and ability to focus on one thing and one thing only. When Mr. Schilke stepped to the line, Dale could see him slow his breathing.

"How can they act so relaxed with all this noise and pressure?" Dale asked his father.

"It takes practice to get good at ignoring outside influences or distractions. Notice they always do the same thing before each shot. They have practiced so much that they are able to repeat the steps without thinking. Just like we talked about when we practice the self-defense moves in the garage. Practice until you don't have to think so you can focus all your energy on the task at hand."

"I'm amazed that all of these techniques are so related."

"Don't be. You'll find out that the secret to success in most areas is related to practice and learning to focus."

At the end of the round, the targets were scored, and the winner was announced. Mr. Garrett had beaten Mr. Schilke by two points. The two men shook hands after receiving their trophies, and the crowd gathered to congratulate the two men.

Dale and his father waited until most of the crowd had dissipated before going up to Mr. Schilke.

"What did you think, Dale? Exciting, wasn't it?"

"I can't believe how you're able to shoot so well under pressure."

"Practice makes perfect. But, today I came close. Now, I'll reflect on my performance and adjust for the next time."

"Second isn't bad."

"Probably not, considering I just lost to the winner of the national championship. You can't beat the best if you don't compete against the best."

Dale's father offered congratulations as he shook his hand. "When you are finished, why doesn't Dale ride with you, so he can show you the way to our house?"

Dale helped Mr. Schilke clean his pistols and pack up. Then they hopped in the car and rumbled down the country roads to Libertyville.

"Dale, tell me how you came to play the cornet."

Dale started from the beginning with learning to play the bugle and ended with his preparation for the upcoming audition for chairs. Mr. Schilke listened quietly.

"It sounds to me like you have had quite a journey learning to play the cornet. I'm looking forward to helping you perfect your abilities."

They arrived at the Kingston home and were greeted by cold roast beef sandwiches with crisp lettuce, cheddar cheese, and Dale's grandmother's chicken and dumpling soup. The conversation was lively, since everyone was interested in Mr. Schilke's background and how he came to be the first-chair trumpet player in the Chicago Symphony. Dale was fascinated that not only was Mr. Schilke a professional trumpet player, but he was also a sportsman, tool and die maker, and he designed and made trumpets and mouthpieces.

Grandmother urged Mr. Schilke to take another piece of apple pie. "If I eat another thing, I'll not be able to play my trumpet, let alone give Dale a lesson. That was one of the best chicken and dumpling soups I've ever had." Grandmother blushed at the compliment.

"Dale, if you and Mr. Schilke want to get started, you may be excused."

Dale led the way to the living room where his horn, two chairs, and music stand were already set up.

Lesson 3

"Is this the cornet Mr. Greenleaf gave you for saving the Conn factory?"

"Sure is. It's beautiful, don't you think? It's a gold-plated Connqueror model 48 A. It's not a trumpet, but I'll get one of those when I start playing in the orchestra in high school."

"No need to rush into getting a trumpet. This cornet will do just fine. Let me see what size mouthpiece you are using."

"I didn't know mouthpieces came in sizes."

Mr. Schilke opened one of the method books he brought to a diagram of a trumpet mouthpiece. He explained the functions for the different parts of a mouthpiece and how finding one that fits your facial features and desired performance needs will help you play better.

Mouthpiece Anatomy

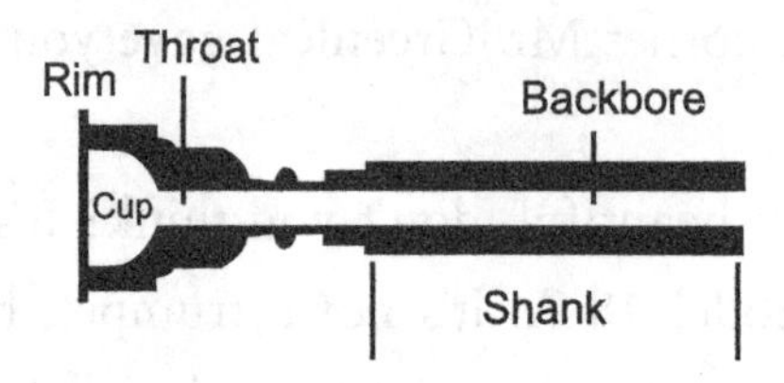

Rim

Wide: Increases endurance.

Narrow: Improves flexibility.

Round: Improves comfort.

Sharp: Increases prescision of attack

Cup

Large: Increases volume, control.

Small: Relieves fatigue, weakness.

Deep: Darkens tone, especially in low register.

Shallow: Brightens tone, improves response, especially in high register.

Throat

Large: Increases blowing freedom, volume, tone; sharpens high register (largest sizes also sharpen low register).

Small: Increases resistance, endurance, brilliance; flattens high register.

Backbore

Combinations of size and shape make the tone darken or brighter, raise or lower the pitch in one or more registers, increase or decrease volume. The backbore's effect depends, in part, upon the throat and cup.

"I learned acoustics when I was studying trumpet in Brussels, Belgium."

"What's acoustics?"

"To make a long story short, acoustics is a branch of physics that deals with sound and sound waves. I see you're playing on a 5Bw. I think I can make you a new mouthpiece and bring it with me next time. But, for now, this will do."

"You're going to make me one?"

"Yes, I work part-time for a small mouthpiece maker. I'll see if I can custom make one for you based upon the mouthpiece used by another great Chicago Symphony trumpet player, Edward Llewellyn."

During the lesson, Dale buzzed his lips, learned new breathing exercises, and worked on the fundamentals of tone, posture, and tonguing. He played a variety of scales and technical studies from his lesson books.

"I've brought a few extra method books that will supplement your current books. It'll be at least a month before I come back, so I've written out four complete lessons and assigned some exercises. Do one each week, and always work on your breathing."

Dale set his cornet carefully in the case. "So we get to have another lesson in a month? I thought this was a one-time lesson."

Mr. Schilke smiled. "After hearing you play and your uncanny ability to listen and apply what I asked you to do, it would be my pleasure to return for another lesson."

Dale's father poked his head in the doorway. "Sounds to me as though Dale has really improved during your short time together."

Mr. Schilke stood up to shake father's hand. "I'd better get going so I can be back by dark. Once that sun goes down, those deer around here will come out. I don't want to hit one, like your band teacher, Mr. Jeffrey."

"How do you know him?'

"That's a story he can tell," Mr. Schilke said as Dale opened the front door. To his surprise, the gang was sitting on the porch.

Sandra stepped forward to shake Mr. Schilke's hand. "I play trumpet with Dale. When we heard you were coming to give him a lesson, we decided to sneak up here and listen to what you said so we could learn something."

Dale introduced his friends one by one and explained what instrument they played. P.J. was the last to be introduced.

"You wouldn't be the kid wearing pajamas who helped save the town, would you? And you wouldn't be the same kid who almost missed the train after getting Arnold Jacobs's signature at the Ravinia concert, would you?"

"Right on both accounts. Nice to meet you, Mr. Schilke."

"We're still laughing about watching you and Arnold running through the concert pavilion." Mr. Schilke turned to Dale. "The next time I come, what do you say I give your friends a master class after your private lesson?" The gang cheered!

Dale walked Mr. Schilke to his car. After the car pulled away, Dale ran back to the porch to join his friends.

Victor suggested, "It's only three o'clock. Why don't we ride out to the quarry for a late afternoon swim?"

He bounded down the stairs of the porch and jumped on his bike. "Last one there is a rotten egg!"

Chapter 12

SABOTAGE

Dale lay awake in his bed, the full moon illuminating the room. Tomorrow, the last day before Thanksgiving break, he would audition once again for chairs. He had messed up his first audition in the spring when Jim Petris distracted him by peering through the window of the band room during his last sight-reading test. As he stared at the ceiling, he fingered each audition piece and thought about how he would avoid being distracted again. A soft whimper came from Scout who was at the foot of his bed, panting and moving his paws as if running in his dreams. Dale reached down and patted Scout.

"Scout ... it's OK, boy." Scout raised his head slightly, looking at Dale before flopping back down. "It looks like both of us are restless tonight."

Scout usually didn't sleep inside, but lately the dog seemed to be more tired than usual. Even his dad and mom had noticed a change and allowed Scout to sleep inside when the weather turned cold.

"Maybe if I sleep down here with you, we can both relax and fall asleep," Dale said, moving his blankets to the end of the bed and resting his head on Scout's soft fur. Scout put a paw on his master's chest as a sign of affection. Dale's last thoughts as he fell asleep were: *You're the best, Scout; the best friend a boy could have.*

The next thing Dale knew, he could smell fresh coffee brewing. His door opened gently, and his father appeared. "I brought you some coffee and let you sleep since today is your audition. I thought we could skip one day of exercise."

Dale raised the steaming cup to his nose and inhaled. "Thanks for letting me sleep in. I didn't sleep so well at first, but once I put my head on Scout for my pillow, I slept like a baby."

After breakfast, the gang walked to school, sharing how each of their auditions had gone. Chrissy had moved up two chairs to fourth chair, first flute. Victor moved up one chair to third chair, second-part French horn. Karl moved up to second chair, first-part trombone. Bobby moved two chairs to eighth chair, first-part clarinet. Tommy beat Bridget to get third chair, first-part saxophone. P.J. stayed the same at fourth chair, saying that chairs didn't matter in the tuba section, since they all played the same part. Dave got to move from mallets to snare. He informed the group that the percussionists technically didn't have chairs because they stood and were assigned parts based upon their individual abilities to play the different percussion instruments.

"I don't think it's fair that Dale and I are the last ones to audition. Why are the trumpets last? It's as though Mr. Jeffrey is tormenting us."

Dale agreed with Sandra. "I'll be glad when it's over. What time is your audition?"

"I'm right after second period during my study hall. What about you?"

"Since I don't have a study hall, I'm playing after school at four o'clock. Do you believe I'm the last one in the entire band to audition?"

"Maybe Mr. Jeffrey is saving the best for last," Chrissy added giving him a soft punch in the shoulder.

"Don't tell that to the rest of the trumpet players, and especially Mr. Jim "Grumpy Pants" Petris." Everyone laughed.

"Did you just call Jim, Grumpy Pants? Where did that nickname come from?" P.J. asked.

"I just made it up. It seemed to fit with him being crabby and getting his pants pocket torn off by Scout. But, don't call him that to his face. It will set him off, and who knows what he'll do."

During the remainder of the walk, the gang told Sandra and Dale about the sight-reading, the order of the scales and etudes they played, hoping to get them to relax before the auditions. As they approached the steps of the school, Bobby spied Jim Petris walking in the front door.

In a loud voice, he said, "Hey, Dale! There's Mr. Grumpy Pants!"

Behind him, Bobby heard an angry voice. "What did you just say?" He turned to face Adrianne. "Did you just call Jim Mr. Grumpy Pants?" she said loudly.

Bobby sputtered, "No, I said Mr. Greenbanks ... you misheard me."

Adrianne was not convinced. "I don't think so. You called Jim Petris Mr. Grumpy Pants. Although I must admit he is rather grumpy, you just better make sure he doesn't know that you're calling him that."

After Adrianne left, Bridget leaned over to Bobby and said sarcastically. "Nice job! You'd better not let that happen again. You don't want Dale getting blamed for that nickname."

They arrived at the band room and did their warm-ups. The rehearsal went quickly, since they could play straight through the holiday concert music now that they had worked out the problem parts. Dale enjoyed playing without stopping because it allowed him to focus on the music. He also didn't have to interact with Jim as often.

At the end of rehearsal, Mr. Jeffrey reminded the trumpets of their audition times. He encouraged the students to take their music and instruments home for the Thanksgiving holiday. As the students put their instruments away in the instrument room, Chrissy could overhear Adrianne's conversation with Jim Petris, even though they were several lockers away. She thought she heard Adrianne say Mr. Grumpy Pants as she glanced in Dale's direction. Jim's face turned red with anger, and he stepped toward Dale who was bent over putting his horn in his locker.

Before Jim got to Dale's locker, Chrissy stepped in, grabbed Dale's arm and laughingly said, "Come on, big fella. Why don't you walk me to class?" Dale quickly slammed the locker door, and before he could check the lock, Chrissy ushered him out of the locker room and into the hallway.

"Sorry I did that," she said and proceeded to explain Jim's reaction to the conversation she just overheard.

"I wondered why you were laughing and dragging me out of the locker room. Thanks, but I hope you're wrong."

Chrissy stopped in front of her math classroom. "Me, too, but stay on your toes and watch out for him."

For the remainder of the day in each of his classes, Dale pretended to pay attention, while he was running over the etudes and scales in his head and repeating the rules for sight-reading. During each passing period, he kept his eyes open for Jim and possible trouble, but he didn't see him. Dale knew that Jim had already played his audition, so at least he wouldn't see him in the band room after school before his tryout. When the last bell rang, Dale lingered at his hall locker until most of the other students had left and worked his way cautiously to the band room.

Mr. Jeffrey was in his office with the first of the five remaining trumpet players. Dale got his folder, unlocked his locker and thought, *I don't remember putting my horn away on its side.* Then he reconsidered. *I guess with Chrissy rushing me, I didn't notice.* Dale didn't want to warm up too much before his audition, so he sat in his chair, reviewing his music for breath marks and dynamics. One of the breath marks was in the wrong place, but when he tried to erase it, he noticed the eraser had fallen out. Just then, Mr. Jeffrey's door opened, and the second to last player entered. With one player to go before his tryout, Dale got his horn out, buzzed his lips, but when he blew into his horn, the sound was stuffy. *I must have turned a valve when I oiled them after band,* he thought. Dale unscrewed each valve cap and pulled out the valve, checking to make sure the holes lined up. Still, the air wouldn't flow through the horn. Nervously, he fingered the valves. Mr. Jeffrey's office door opened, and the final student before Dale left.

"Last, but not least. Come in, and let's hear what you can do."

Dale didn't know what to say, so he picked up his horn and music and moved toward the office.

"You look pale ... are you feeling alright?"

Dale plopped in the chair. "I don't know what the problem is," he mumbled. "My horn doesn't work."

Mr. Jeffrey slid into the chair next to Dale. "It worked in band today. I just checked the valves, but it still doesn't work."

Dale handed the cornet to Mr. Jeffrey, who seemed irritated. Mr. Jeffrey tried to blow through the horn, but nothing came out. "That's odd. It can't be the valves because no air is getting through the lead pipe. It's like there's something stuck in there. Were you chewing gum while you were warming up? That could block the lead pipe."

Dale shook his head. "I never play with food or gum in my mouth."

"When did you last clean it?"

"About two weeks ago. I took all the slides and valves out and then flushed water through the horn. Then I put it back together, and it worked right up until about ten minutes ago."

"Hmmm," and Mr. Jeffrey wheeled around in his chair and handed Dale his cornet. "We need to finish these auditions today, so take your mouthpiece out and use mine."

Dale played some long tones and lip slurs, bobbling the notes and having difficulty adapting to a cornet he had never played.

After a long day, Mr. Jeffrey was not sympathetic to Dale's situation. "If you can't keep your horn in working condition, then you have to face the consequences."

For the next fifteen minutes, Dale struggled through the audition, making numerous mistakes. When it came time to sight-read, however, he was able to play all four of the less technically demanding sight-reading exercises.

"I wish you'd played the first part of your tryout like the last part. The sight-reading was great, but the prepared part wasn't what I had expected from you." Dale turned red, and he looked down at the cornet in his lap.

Mr. Jeffrey continued. "It isn't easy to play on a different horn, but sometimes you have to step up to a challenging moment. Today, you didn't. You'll stay second chair to Jim for the next concert."

"I'm sorry I disappointed you, but I still don't understand what happened to my horn. I'll take it home and clean it again over vacation."

As Dale stood up to leave the office, Mr. Jeffrey said, "I don't think you disappointed me. I think you disappointed yourself. Use this audition as a learning experience for your next performance."

Dale was deep in thought as he walked down the deserted hall to the outside door. As he reached for the door handle, he sensed movement. He whirled around to find Jim standing behind him. He'd let his guard down, and now he was alone with his nemesis.

"Tough audition, huh?" Jim taunted. "Sounds like you're still second best." The older boy inched forward until Dale could smell the spearmint flavor of the gum he was snapping ominously. "What's the matter? Can't think of anything to say, like," and Jim raised the pitch of his voice to sound like a girl, "Knock it off, Mr. Grumpy Pants, or maybe you should run and call your little flute player friend who saved you today? She actually has more spine than you do." Jim's face hovered menacingly in front of Dale when the band room door burst open. Mr. Jeffrey came running down the hall carrying a shiny, rope-like object, as Jim slunk into the shadows.

"Dale, I'm glad I caught up with you. I wanted to give you this tool called a snake to run through your horn when you wash it out during vacation." As he came closer, Mr. Jeffrey looked to the side to see Jim leaning against the lockers. "What are you doing here so late? Students aren't supposed to be in the building unless they're with a teacher."

Stepping into the light, Jim stood close to Dale. "I just wanted to make sure that the rest of my section finished their auditions. As section leader, I want to encourage them to do their best. I hope that's OK with you? I was just telling Dale how good he sounded, right, Dale?"

Mr. Jeffrey raised his eyebrow and looked at Dale. "Jim's just being his usual self and giving me some advice." Dale reached over to take the snake from Mr. Jeffrey as the director gave each of them a puzzled look.

Dale was out the door in a flash, running down the street, not stopping until he was within sight of his home.

Chapter 13

First Hunt

Thanksgiving morning dawned with a hard frost covering the ground.

"Why don't you pour yourself and Grandpa one more cup of coffee while I go start the car. It needs to warm up to get the frost off the windshield." Dale shivered as a cold north wind blew in the kitchen when Dad opened the door.

Grandpa took the cup from Dale. "Are you excited about your first hunt? This is a family tradition that goes back to my grandfather's time."

"I have watched you go for years and thought it looked like fun."

"Today, you're done watching. It's time to step up and see if you can outhunt and outshoot your dad and me."

"I think I'm ready, but I'm not sure about the outshoot part. I'm pretty good at the skeet shooting, but with live birds, we'll have to see."

"You'll do fine. Just remember to stay calm and follow the rules and our instructions. Did you pack everything?"

"I think so. Last night, I cleaned the gun and put it in the case. I also laid out my wool hunting pants, long underwear, two pairs of socks, boots, wool sweater, and red plaid hunting jacket and cap. I packed the shells and extra gloves, and Grandma set out some sandwiches and a thermos of hot chocolate. I think I'm ready."

"Sounds like you are. Let's load up. Your dad will have the car all warmed up for us."

The trio drove about thirty minutes to a farm owned by Mr. Star, a distant relative of the Kingstons. Several cars were parked in front of a red barn. A large group of men were huddled around a fire in a big steel drum.

Grandpa waved to the group. "Thanksgiving is a time to renew our friendships. Another part of this traditional hunt is when a young man like you is ready to join the group; everyone welcomes him and reminisces about their first hunt. Remember to stand tall, shoulders back, make eye contact, firmly shake their hands, and introduce yourself if needed. Once we get done with the introductions, we'll head out for the hunt. OK, let's get out and go over to the barn."

Father and Grandfather were greeted with hugs and handshakes. Most of the men had not seen Dale's dad Jake since he went off to war and were very excited to see him. After each person greeted Jake, he would turn and introduce Dale and explain how they were related. The men were friendly, and Dale enjoyed the lively conversations and stories of when they were young and went on their first hunt. Dale followed his father until they had met everyone.

"Now the war is over I'm sure we'll have more family reunions. I'm proud of the way you greeted everyone and made small talk. You've stepped up to the first challenge of the day. We'll have more to come, but just watch, listen, and let these men help you during the hunt."

"I'll make you and Grandfather proud."

Grandfather extended his hand to Dale. "You've already made me proud. From now on, when we're together, call me C.H. All of my friends call me that. And today you're my friend, and a person I can trust."

Dale smiled at his grandfather. "But only when we're alone or hunting. Your grandmother wouldn't approve, but it's time to treat each other like adults."

"What does C.H. stand for?"

Dad laughed. "Those are the initials for his first and middle name, Clarence Howard. He got that nickname years ago on the railroad, and it just stuck."

"OK. C.H. it is." Dale shook C.H.'s hand.

Then his father offered, "I want you to call me Jake when we're out in the field. If you're old enough to hunt, then you're old enough to call me Jake."

"OK, Dad, I mean, Jake."

Mr. Star welcomed the group and explained the details of the hunt and which fields the group would start in. He reminded everyone of the shooting rules and about staying in a straight line, letting the dogs do the work. When he finished, the group moved to their cars for the short drive to the fields.

Once in the car, Jake said, "I want you to hunt between C.H. and me. I've arranged with Mr. Star for you to be in the center of the first field where the shooting will be the easiest. The only difference between this and shooting skeet is that we use dogs. Once the dogs go on point, I'll talk you through the next part about how to approach the pheasant to get it to fly or to flush it out. Remember to call out hen or cock. We don't shoot the hens; they are gray. The cocks are brightly colored red and have a white ring around their necks."

Dale leaned against the front seat. "I'm a little nervous shooting in front of so many other hunters."

"We've all been there. It is just part of growing up. Relax, follow the rules, and listen to C.H. and me, and you'll be just fine."

As Dale got out of the car, his heart began to race. Men were unloading dogs, while others zipped up their warm jackets and removed their guns from the cases, spreading out on the edge of the corn field. The sounds of dogs barking and men talking stopped suddenly once the group formed a single straight line at the end of a long cornfield. Mr. Star shouted, "Load up and move into the field."

Dale put a shell into the gun's chamber. Dad reminded him to watch the dogs, just like they practiced.

The long line of men began to walk slowly in a straight line down the rows of corn stubble while the dogs zigzagged ahead, sniffing out the birds. Off to the right, Dale heard someone shout, "Hold up! Dogs are on one!" He watched the hunter closest to the dog slowly move forward while the other men stayed back. Dale was fascinated how the dog stood perfectly still with its head pointed at a clump of corn stocks. The hunter moved in, gave the stalks a kick, and out flew a big gray pheasant, followed by shouts of "hen, hen." The hunters put their guns down.

"Did you see that, Dale? That's exactly how to do it. Except most of the time, the bird will flush, and you won't have to kick it out."

The line moved again, stopping when the dogs went on point or when the birds would flush. As they approached the end of the first field, the dogs began to work into the middle of the field where Dale was.

"Get ready, Dale," Grandpa advised. "The end of the field is where it gets exciting. The birds will have to flush because they are out of cover. Some might even flush right under your feet without a dog near. Don't shoot anything that's not in front of you. We'll call your name if it's yours."

Dale began walking slowly the last twenty yards of the field. His mouth went dry and his heart raced, but he remembered his training. Take a deep breath, stand straight, and stay focused. Dale snapped his head to the right when he heard a sudden thundering of wings, followed by shouts of, "Cock, cock! Dale, take it."

Dale felt as if he were moving in slow motion, just like in band when he had to play a solo for the first time. He could see it all, the bird, his gun, and the dogs. He pulled the gun to his shoulder, as he had done hundreds of times shooting skeet with his father. He aimed and pulled the trigger, feeling the jolting recoil of the gun. There followed a puff of feathers and the bird fell from the sky.

"Dale, reload!" his father commanded as the line of men surged forward. Dale reloaded, as shouts and gunshots rang out, as a flock of pheasants flushed. He was startled when a bird flushed beneath his boot and flew toward his father. "Cock, cock! Dad, take it!" A shotgun blasted, and the bird fell.

Just as fast as the shooting had started, the shooting ended.

"Dale, you got one!" C.H. shouted as he and the other hunters unloaded their shotguns and picked up their birds. Some of the dogs returned with birds in their mouths.

"That happened so fast, I didn't have time to think. I can't believe I got my first pheasant!"

"Not only did you get one, but you called one out for me. Great job!" Jake said.

The men strolled over to shake Dale's hand before heading to the next field. Each time they walked a field, they changed positions so each man got a chance to be in the middle. When the morning hunt ended, they returned to the barn to tally up the birds and take a group photo. Dale and C.H. each had gotten another bird, making their total four for the day.

After the picture, they loaded up their equipment and began the drive home. Dale never stopped talking all the way home. As they pulled up to the house, he leaned over the seat.

"Thanks, Jake and C.H., for taking me."

Dad put the car in park and looked back at his son. "You really stepped up today. Now, out you go. Get those birds out of the trunk and show your mother and grandma."

Dale jumped out of the car as his mom and grandma came out the back door to greet the returning hunters.

Dale opened the trunk, grabbing the four pheasants by the feet, and held them up. "Look, I got two, C.H. got one, and Jake got one. What do you think?"

Mother furrowed her brow. "I think two things. One, you had a successful hunt, and two, you're now calling your dad and grandpa by their first names."

Dale realized his mistake, but his mom gave Jake a big hug and said, "I guess all of my men were successful today. Let's go bake these pheasants in sour cream." Then she glanced back at Dale. "But don't think you're going to start calling me Ruth."

Dale laughed. "No way! You'll always be Mom to me."

Chapter 14

ANSWERS

"Morning, Dale," his grandfather said as he entered the kitchen. "Are you as full as I am from yesterday's Thanksgiving meal? I'm not sure I can eat breakfast, I'm so full."

"I was so full this morning I couldn't run very fast. Even Scout could keep up."

"How's Scout feeling these days?"

"He seems to have good days and bad. Today he was able to run with me the whole time. So, I feel better about him not being so tired."

"That dog went through a lot last year, after escaping the dog trainers and traveling five hundred miles during a Montana winter. I'm sure it took a toll on him."

"You don't think Scout is sick do you?"

"No, but he might just be getting old. We'll watch him over the next few months, and if he doesn't get better, we'll take him to the vet. But let's not worry about that now. What's on your agenda today?"

"After breakfast, I'm going to clean my cornet before going to Sandra's for a quintet practice."

"I thought you cleaned it a couple of weeks ago."

Dale hadn't thought about the audition and the confrontation with Jim, but his grandfather's question brought it all back. "Well, I did clean it recently, but lately it seems to be playing stuffy."

Dale changed the subject. "The best part of the day will be that we're going over to Mr. Edwards's house after the practice to listen to some more jazz recordings. We've gone there four times so far this fall and learned a lot."

"I can't think of anyone who knows more about jazz or has a better record collection than him."

Grandpa then reminded Dale not to let the water get too hot when cleaning his cornet, because it could take the finish off.

"I'll be careful," he said, heading upstairs to get his horn. Mr. Jeffrey had shown the brass players how to clean their horns in the bathtub by first putting down a towel in the tub so the horn wouldn't get scratched. Then, Dale took the valves and slides out of the horn and set them on the towel. He ran enough lukewarm water to cover the cornet and its parts. After the tub was full, Dale waited while the horn soaked in the water to loosen any dirt in the pipes. He thought about the audition and his poor performance. *How could I have worked so hard and then had my horn fail me? It doesn't make sense. My locker was locked. The horn worked fine in band that morning.*

Dale leaned over the tub and began running water and then pushing the wire snake through each slide. Dale found nothing in the slides, so he began to flush out the lead pipe. Holding the horn under the bathtub faucet, the water should have gone in one end and out the other with ease. Instead, the water just bubbled back. Puzzled, Dale held the pipe up to the light and tried to look through it. Something was preventing him from seeing straight through. Taking the snake, he carefully threaded the wire into the lead pipe. It only went about an inch and stopped. He knew better than to try and force it farther, so he removed the snake and tried the other end.

Again, Dale slid the snake into the horn. This time, it went in about six inches before stopping at an obstruction. Dale pushed the wire harder with no luck, so he decided to run water in the pipe at the same time he pushed the wire in, hoping the two would dislodge whatever was in there. After several failed attempts, the obstruction started to move little by little down the pipe. With one final push, out it came, landing in the tub of water. Dale couldn't tell what it was, so he picked it up and washed it off, revealing a soft pink object. Dale's heart began to pound, as he flashed back to his cornet case on its side and the pencil with no eraser. It all began to make sense.

There was only one way the eraser got in his horn. JIM! It had to be that when Chrissy rushed him out of the equipment room, his locker didn't lock, and Jim sabotaged his horn with the only thing available, the eraser from their folder.

Dale oiled his valves and greased his slides before putting his cornet back together. When the last slide was in place, it was time to test it. He took a breath and out came the notes as smooth and round as they had ever been. Rolling the eraser between his fingers, Dale vowed, *OK, Jim! It's time for me to erase the past.*

Chapter 15

LIVE JAZZ IS BETTER

The quintet played the last phrase of "Sonata" from *Die Bankelsangerlieder.* They had practiced adding dynamics and emotion all morning, and the results of the ensemble's hard work were evident. P.J.'s driving bass line, combined with Victor's French horn, and Karl's trombone countermelody, were adding the harmonic support to the melody provided by Sandra and Dale. The players focused on playing their individual parts. When the group reached the final note, all eyes were on Dale, waiting for the bob of his cornet bell as the signal to cut off. Dale waited just to the point where the group could no longer *crescendo* and dipped his horn. The group stopped, remaining silent; the look on their faces told the story. They had just played the entire piece straight through from memory and without having to stop.

"Bravo, bravo," they heard coming from outside the front door of Sandra's house.

"Come in," Sandra yelled as Chrissy, Tommy, Dave, Bridget, and Bobby burst through the door. Bridget surveyed the scene.

"Where's your music, and why are you standing instead of sitting?"

Sandra explained, "After working out all the problem spots with the music, Dale suggested we try the piece from memory."

"That way we could concentrate on the emotion and dynamics," P.J. added.

"But, why are you standing?" Bobby asked.

"Last week my parents took me to hear the Salvation Army Band concert in Terra Haute. They had a quintet similar to ours that moved around the stage as they played," Victor said proudly.

Sandra's mom interrupted the discussion. "Lunch is ready. I hope you like toasted cheese sandwiches with tomato soup."

The conversation at lunch was lively because the members of the gang were sharing their Thanksgiving experiences. Dale was the last to go.

Chrissy listened carefully to the vivid description of the hunting trip. "Two pheasants? I wish I could've gone. I'd love to see the dogs flushing the birds."

Bridget adamantly disagreed. "Why would you shoot those beautiful birds? They don't have a chance against dogs and guns."

"Come on, Bridget," Dale reasoned. "You eat chickens, steers, lamb, fish, and who knows what else, and they're all living things. The only difference is you didn't shoot them. But, somebody had to slaughter them."

"Either way, I'm jealous and want to go sometime. Could you ask your dad?" Chrissy pleaded.

"Maybe during Christmas vacation. With the way you shoot, you'll do fine. Did you know your dad and mine have hunted together since they were kids?"

"Even more reason for us to hunt together."

Bridget, tired of the hunting conversation, looked at her watch and stood up. "Sorry to interrupt you two, but we told Mr. Edwards we'd be over at one. I don't want to be late."

Mr. Edwards lived in a modest bungalow on MacArthur Street, one of Dale's favorite parts of town because it had a boulevard in the middle, giving the neighborhood a park-like feeling. The walk to his house took about twenty minutes and the final block was uphill. Climbing the steps to his house, the gang was out of breath and gasping for air.

Before they could ring the doorbell, Mr. Edwards opened the large wooden door. "I heard all this gasping and wheezing and knew you were here."

"We wouldn't be all out of breath if Victor hadn't said, 'Last one to the porch is a rotten egg.'" None of us wanted to be a rotten egg, so we ran extra fast," Dale explained while shaking Mr. Edwards's hand.

"Who lost?"

"Me, as usual," P.J. said, bringing up the rear. "I'm always last."

"You may be last in running, but you're first in our hearts," Chrissy purred, which caused P.J.'s face to redden.

Mr. Edwards urged the boys and girls to sit down while he brought out refreshments from the kitchen. Sitting in his easy chair, he said, "Catch me up on how jazz band and basketball tryouts are going. It's been several weeks since my last update, and I might have some recordings of the tunes you are practicing." Mr. Edwards had a fire roaring in the fireplace.

"May I sit next to the fire and warm up my hands?" Sandra asked.

Dave scooted next to Sandra on the hearth. "You know what they say, 'Cold hands, warm heart.'"

Sandra fluttered her eyelashes. "That's so sweet. I don't think I've heard that before."

Mr. Edwards leaned back in his chair. "Did you make the basketball team, Dale?"

"Victor and I were the only seventh graders to make the team. The eighth graders are really good, so we're not getting much playing time. We're trying to learn the plays, zones, and man-to-man defenses the eighth graders already know. The season will really pick up after Christmas vacation. That's when we begin to play all our conference games. Until then, we'll be practicing a lot and having scrimmages with other schools."

"When you play West Libertyville, be sure to tell me. I'll be there. When I was going to East Liberty, we had quite the rivalry. I still don't like them, and that was twenty years ago.

So tell me how jazz band is going. The last time you were here, you were just getting ready for tryouts."

Bridget set her drink down and began. "Well, I think we represented Emerson Grade School fairly well. I made second alto sax and Tommy got second tenor. We represent two of the five sax players. P.J. and another eighth grader named Felix share the bass part, but P.J. is the only bass player in the combo. Dave is the backup drummer, Karl is playing bass bone, or fourth part, and Sandra and Dale made the trumpet section."

"Dale, what part do you play? Did you get the lead part?"

"No, I'm not a lead player," and Mr. Edwards quickly added, "yet." Dale continued, "The lead has to be able to play high notes and be very aggressive. I'm more of a soloist and section player. I got the second part that does most of the soloing, and Sandra is playing the fourth part."

"Who's the lead player?"

"His name is Jim Petris." Dale hesitated before adding, "He's kind of mean and pushy, so he makes a good lead player."

Sandra broke in, "Yeah, good lead, but terrible section leader. He's very rude and kind of a bully."

"Why does that name sound familiar to me? You said Jim Petris, right? I know that name for some reason." Mr.

Edwards scratched his short black hair as if it would help him remember.

"Now, tell me what tunes you're playing." He stood up and moved to the wooden storage cabinets lining the walls, filled with record albums. "Let me see if I have any recordings of the songs."

For the next few hours, the gang called out the titles of the songs they had in their folders. Each member had a favorite chart. Karl liked *It Don't Mean a Thing* by Louis Armstrong and Duke Ellington. Dave liked *Sing, Sing, Sing* by Benny Goodman because of the drum solo. Bridget liked *Mini the Moocher* by Cab Calloway.

Mr. Edwards had several different recordings of groups playing the songs and talked about how each version is a little different, which is what makes jazz so much fun to play and listen to.

"Do you notice that although I played the same song by two different bands, each group takes the same song and puts its own twist to it?"

"I can't get over how different the solos are in the two songs," Sandra said.

Mr. Edwards became very animated. "It's even more exciting to hear a jazz soloist live. They never play the solo the same. One time they may play very melodically, and the next time they play the solo with different rhythmic inflections or with a variety of melodic ideas that develop during the solo. Jazz live is definitely better."

"Do you think you can take us to hear some live jazz?" Dave asked.

"Live jazz in Libertyville is hard to find. I usually go to Chicago, to the clubs on the South Side, to hear live jazz."

"I don't know if my mom will let me go to Chicago again after what happened on our last trip to Chicago," Bridget said.

"I remember that day and the expressions on your faces when you came into the dining car after Mr. Jeffrey missed the train. You sure looked scared. But for now, let's start with listening to records in my house. Then maybe, and I mean maybe, we can figure some type of trip to hear some live jazz. Let's end with one of my favorites, *Groovin High* by Dizzy Gillespie.

When the last recording was finished, they each thanked Mr. Edwards and headed home. It was close to five o'clock when they left, and the late November sky was already darkening. The temperature was falling as Chrissy and Dale trudged up Simpson Hill. "My hands are freezing," complained Chrissy.

"Remember, cold hands mean a warm heart," Dale joked, taking her hand in his. "Here, put your hands under my coat." Putting his arm around her shoulders, he pulled her close.

"That feels a lot better," she said as she snuggled close to Dale. "You always seem to look out for me."

"I think lately you've been the one looking out for me."

Chrissy looked up at Dale, surprised at his confession.

During the remainder of the walk, Chrissy listened intently as Dale filled her in on what happened after she hustled him away from Jim in the band locker room. Dale told it all, beginning with the locker not locking and the disastrous audition. By the time Dale described the final event of finding the eraser in his horn, Chrissy was fuming.

"You have to tell someone about this. I don't like where this is headed. I don't trust Jim ... I'm scared just thinking about what else he could do."

Dale squeezed Chrissy's shoulder and comforted her. "He's not going to hurt us. He's tough, but I believe he is more bark than bite."

Stopping in mid-stride, Chrissy pulled away from Dale and faced him. "I hope you're right, but I'm warning you. If he does anything else, I'm going to tell Mr. Jeffrey—like it or not."

"Geez, I hope I don't ever make you mad!" Pulling her back under his arm, he said, "Give me your hands so I can warm them up. I think your heart is already warm."

Chrissy snuggled back against Dale, both falling silent, deep in thought.

Chapter 16

REDEMPTION

Dale and his dad carried the last mattress from the garage and dropped it on the basement floor. "Whew! Those are heavy and awkward. That was a workout in itself," Dale said, flopping down on one of the mattresses.

"At least for the next several months, we'll be warm while working out. I think with the enormous amount of running you're doing in basketball and with the cold, snow, and ice, we won't run in the mornings. Instead, we'll focus on strength training exercises and self-defense. What do you say?"

"I think Scout will be glad. The cold really seems to be bothering him lately. I've noticed he's limping by the time we get home."

Dad slid one of the mattresses toward the center. "Last year was hard on him."

"That's what Grandpa said."

"Don't worry about Scout. He's one tough dog," Dad said as they went back upstairs.

Three weeks had passed since Thanksgiving. The Christmas concert would be in five days followed by the two-week Christmas break, and the students at East Libertyville were restless. Mr. Jeffrey stood on the podium and didn't start the warm-up as usual.

"Quiet, please. Before we begin our warm-up, Principal Hamilton will make several announcements to the student body. Let's sit quietly while he's making his announcements."

The intercom clicked, followed by four musical notes played on a set of bells.

"Good morning, students," began Mr. Hamilton. "Over the past several weeks, the faculty and staff have noticed a change in student behavior as we enter the holiday season. Being young and excited is fine, but being loud in the hallways and, at times, disruptive to our educational atmosphere is not. Our code of conduct will be strictly enforced, and if needed, detentions and other forms of discipline will be used. Be respectful of one another and control your excitement for the upcoming events. Remember, we have a great tradition at East Libertyville, and we need your help in making the last few days educationally productive. Thanks ... and go Lions. RRROOOOOOOOOOAAARR."

Bridget rolled her eyes at Sandra, which Mr. Jeffrey ignored. "I'd like to add a few comments. We've worked hard getting ready for our first concert. With just five rehearsals left, we still have several soloists to select, as well as continuing to add dynamics and emotion to our playing. I want our section leaders to lead by example and help each member of their sections in any way needed." He picked up his baton to start the chorale.

The band worked on the opening march *Pepita Greus*. Dale had practiced the opening solos, and Mr. Jeffrey had narrowed the soloist to either Dale or Jim. Dale had managed to minimize his contact with Jim after the auditions, while Jim had backed off, except for an occasional snotty remark directed at Dale. Chrissy hadn't told anyone about what Jim had done. Dale wouldn't confront Jim about sabotaging his instrument until the time was right. Jim must have noticed the change, but he continued to act as if nothing had happened.

Mr. Jeffrey stopped the band at the end of the march and faced the trumpet section. "Let's get the trumpet solos decided today before moving on next Monday to the selection of the flute, French horn, and clarinet soloists. I want to pick the soloist for the march and also the soloist for *Colonial Song* by Percy Grainger. Whoever plays the best today will keep the solo and play it at the concert. This will alleviate some of the tension in the trumpet section. Give me a second to tune the flutes, and then we'll start."

Mr. Jeffrey turned to Adrianne and had her play a C, followed by the other members of the section. Dale sensed Jim staring at him, so he closed his eyes, shut out all the sounds around him, and focused on how he would play the solos.

Dale's concentration was broken when Jim leaned over and whispered, "I can't wait to watch you clutch like you did at your auditions. You do remember you messed up two different times. Get ready for mess up numbers three and four."

Dale realized that it was the time to take on Jim. As Jim turned forward, Dale leaned over, reached into his shirt, pulling out Scout's two dog tags that he always wore on a chain around his neck.

"I don't think so, Jim. I know what you did and how you did it. Does this look familiar?" Dale said as he held up a pink eraser dangling on the chain with the dog tags. Jim's face turned white. "I think, Jim, it's time I erased the past and show you what a real leader plays like." Keeping eye contact with Jim, Dale leaned back into his chair and put the dog tags and eraser back under his shirt.

"Now that we've fixed the flute intonation issue, let's hear the trumpets. Jim, why don't you go first?"

Jim didn't respond. After a brief hesitation, Jim's voice cracked, "Sorry, Mr. Jeffrey. I'm ready when you are."

"Are you sure? You seem a bit disoriented."

Dale interrupted. "Mr. Jeffrey, if Jim isn't ready, I can play."

"That's nice of you, Dale, but as section leader Jim should go first."

Jim glared at Dale and brought his trumpet up to his lips. Mr. Jeffrey gave the downbeat, and Jim started, but after playing the first two notes, he bobbled the next note, and missed the E-flat in the quintuplet.

Mr. Jeffrey stopped the band, his face showing no emotion. "OK, Dale, your turn." Dale leaned forward to empty his spit and whispered to Jim, "Erase the past." Dale sat up tall and took a deep breath, just like the first time he played the solo and during pheasant hunting, where everything seemed to be in slow motion. He could hear Mr. Schilke's words of wisdom about concentration and focus. Mr. Jeffrey gave the downbeat, and Dale began playing just like he had imagined and practiced. He played the solo with no mistakes.

Pepita Greus

Mr. Jeffrey stopped the band. "There's no need to hear more. Dale, you get the first solo in the march. Now let's move onto *Colonial Song*. Dale, you play first this time."

Dale looked at Jim and put his hand on the tags through his shirt. He smiled slightly and waited for the downbeat.

Dale played better than the first time, while Jim, feeling the pressure, made several simple mistakes.

Mr. Jeffrey, unaware of the deeper meaning of his words, said, "Dale, you played as though you were trying to erase the memory of your earlier auditions."

Dale glanced at Chrissy who smiled back hearing the words "*erase your earlier auditions.*" Their secret was safe between them. No one else, except Jim, had a clue what had happened.

Mr. Jeffrey closed his scores. "Before dismissing you, I want to thank you for applying yourself today and staying calm. Please continue this behavior throughout the day. See you Monday."

Dale jumped up and squeezed down the row to talk with Sandra. Before the rehearsal started, he'd placed his cornet case in the back of the band room to avoid the instrument locker room and any contact with Jim. When he saw Jim go into the instrument locker room, he put his horn away and headed to the door of the band room to wait for the bell.

Chrissy ran over to Dale and squeezed his hand, whispering, "Congratulations! You should've seen Jim's face when you showed him the eraser."

Dale didn't answer as he warily watched the door to the locker room. He could see Adrianne consoling Jim on the other side of the room. The two made eye contact, and Dale didn't like what he saw. He saw a deep sense of rage in Jim's smoldering eyes. Dale wondered: *What have I started*? He averted his eyes. The bell rang, and he scurried off to his next class with Chrissy at his side.

Chapter 17

STRATEGY

Dale was relieved that the solo auditions had gone so well. It began to dawn on him, however, that beating Jim for the solos was only the beginning. He would have to step up to the challenge of playing the solos perfectly at the Christmas concert in front of a large audience to prove why he had earned the right to play them. Scout gave Dale a lick on Dale's face as if saying, *Come on ... snap out of it ... you'll do fine.*

Dale hugged Scout back. "I can always count on you to keep me focused." Scout barked twice and rolled on his back, wanting a belly scratch as a reward.

Dale scratched Scout extra hard, adding, "I sure am glad you're feeling better." Dale heard the slam of a car door and looked out the window to see Mr. Schilke getting out of a black two-door Buick.

He grabbed his horn and earplugs, called good-bye to his mother, and ran down the steps to meet his mentor, just as he was coming up the sidewalk for today's shooting and cornet lesson.

Dale climbed into the front seat. Mr. Schilke told him about his busy week with the symphony. "I'm looking forward to taking a break from performing to get outside for a change. Having a hobby such as shooting clears my head. Do you know Handel's *Messiah*?"

"Is that the one with the choir and orchestra, when the audience stands during the last song?"

"That's the one. Tomorrow I have to play it on a D piccolo trumpet. It's a demanding piece because you sit for a long time and then have to play these very high, difficult trumpet parts with no warm-up. Lots of pressure since the audience knows the piece so well."

"What's a D piccolo trumpet? I thought all trumpets were in B-flat."

"Band cornets and trumpets are, but orchestra parts are written for trumpets in the key of C, D, and sometimes B-flat. To make a long story short, it depends upon the notes of the piece. If a part is really high, then a small trumpet such as a D trumpet allows the player to play those notes more easily. I brought the D trumpet with me, so I can show you during our lesson."

Dale looked at the passing cornfields, the cornstalks lying haphazardly over the frozen fields. After thinking a moment, he said, "But did you say you felt a lot of pressure to perform well this Sunday? I didn't think a famous player like you would feel pressure during a concert."

"Some concerts have more pressure than others, but remember, I'm expected to play flawlessly. You aren't first chair in the Chicago Symphony, one of the greatest symphonies in the world, without high expectations from the conductor and the audience. It goes with the job. Learning how to deal with pressure is the secret. I've known great players who couldn't perform under pressure and quit the profession."

"How did you learn to deal with it?"

"I'll teach you, but then you'll have to find your own way of handling these types of situations." Mr. Schilke stopped the car in front of the shooting range and turned off the motor. "Before we begin, I want you to think of everything we do in life like this. If you're going to live this life, which is the only choice you have, then live it as though you were a lion, because living rabbit-like won't change anything."

Dale wasn't sure what that meant, but he jumped out of the car, eager for another shooting lesson.

For the next hour, the two took turns shooting at the targets and scoring them. Mr. Schilke was a master teacher, and with each suggestion, Dale was able to connect it to playing the trumpet or other aspects of life.

"Are all the situations in life, and how we handle them, related?" Dale asked as they put away their guns in the trunk of the car.

"Well, Dale, I don't know for certain. But what I do know is that life is full of choices and hard work. Nothing comes easily to most of us, but having the ability to make good choices and deal with adversity when it arises is the key to success."

"I think I get it, although I'm only twelve. I've been tested lately with some tough situations," Dale admitted.

"The first step to success starts with recognizing a problem and what your choices are." Mr. Schilke opened the car door for Dale. "Let's get a bite to eat before we have our music lesson. Can you show me the way to a place called Dobbins's Diner? I hear they serve a mighty fine tenderloin sandwich."

Soon they pulled in front of a low-slung building painted white with blue trim. Dale introduced him to the owner, Mr. Dobbins.

"Glad to meet you, Mr. Schilke." He whisked the two to a seat in a booth next to the front window. Dale ordered the usual.

"If the usual is a tenderloin and a chocolate malt, then I'll have the same. Dale says they're the best in the whole world."

Dale watched as Mr. Dobbins bee-lined toward the kitchen with their order. As his eyes surveyed the rest of the diner, he noticed a familiar face. Jim was sitting in the corner booth with a short, older red-haired woman. Jim gave Dale a menacing look before turning back to the conversation he was having with the woman.

Mr. Schilke turned to see what Dale was looking at. "Do you know that young man? He seems to be staring at you." Dale explained that Jim did know him and that they had had several run-ins, especially since Dale had earned the right to play several solos.

"I knew a boy like that when I was young, and he bullied me. I sure learned a lot about myself having to deal with him."

Dale looked at this older man who seemed so accomplished and confident. "You were bullied?"

"I think everyone has been intimidated by someone at some time in their life. As a young person, I, too, was bullied, probably because I was small and very talented. But, tell me more about what's going on between you and Jim."

Dale opened up about his problems starting with his initial audition at East Libertyville. Halfway through lunch, Jim and the red-haired lady left through the side door, much to the relief of Dale.

Mr. Schilke listened sympathetically. "During our music lesson today, I'll help you learn to channel your emotions into your playing and prevent them from affecting your performances."

"By the way, where are we going for the lesson?"

"Let me pay the bill, and I'll show you."

They headed down the street that went by East Libertyville Junior High. Mr. Schilke wheeled the car into the school parking lot.

"Why are we stopping? I think the school is locked."

"You're right—you can't take me in, but I can take you in."

Dale picked up his backpack containing his horn and music, while Mr. Schilke took out his trumpet case and bag of music. They headed to the side door next to the stage.

Dale looked up at him with awe. "I've never gone in this door before, but I think it leads to the auditorium where our Christmas concert will be this week."

"I think you're right," he said pulling the metal door open for Dale. Dale put his hand to his forehead to shade his eyes from the bright lights. "Is that you, Mr. Jeffrey?"

"I'm over here putting the last chairs and stands in place for this week's rehearsals." Mr. Jeffrey strode to the pair and shook Mr. Schilke's hand vigorously.

Mr. Schilke explained why he had brought Dale to the junior high. "I thought that if you could practice in the same auditorium as the concert, you wouldn't be as nervous when it came time for the actual concert. I do this myself sometimes in Orchestra Hall. I sit alone onstage and play my parts, imagining that the orchestra is playing to an auditorium filled with people."

Mr. Jeffrey excused himself to write program notes for the concert in his office. Mr. Schilke took out his gleaming silver trumpet as he outlined the details of the lesson. "Dale, I want you to sit in the same chair as you do in band. I'll sit where, what is the first-chair kid's name again?"

"You mean Jim?"

"Yes, I'll sit where Jim sits."

Dale moved down the rows, sat in his chair, and motioned to the left. "Jim sits here."

With a flourish, Mr. Schilke plopped on the chair with his legs spread firmly on the ground. Dale arranged his lesson books and the concert music on the stand between them. To warm up, they buzzed their mouthpieces and played long tones.

"No, Dale, you're not filling up your horn with enough air. Remember you're playing in an auditorium that is at least ten times the size of your band room. It takes longer for your sound to bounce off the back wall and come back. You must project more sound by driving the air and filling up the room." Mr. Schilke brought the brilliant trumpet up to his lips and played the opening of *Pepita Greus,* the echo of the last note filling the auditorium and lingering as he set the trumpet on his knee.

Pepita Greus

Dale blinked and looked at his teacher with renewed respect. He had never known that such a powerful sound could come from a single brass instrument.

Dale began to relax and fill his horn with more air, getting used to the size of the room. They worked on the etudes he was assigned, making small changes in technique, but most of the discussion centered on playing out and putting more emotion into his playing.

"Dale, anyone can play the written notes on a page. I don't want notes. I want music, and to an audience that means emotion and expression. That is what gives music its life. Notes are just symbols and mean nothing without you personally making them mean something. Do you understand?"

"Sure, it's kind of like a poem I learned from my grandfather called *Flanders Fields*. The words on the page mean nothing, if you don't know the history and meaning behind the words. Plus, when you read the words, you have to give certain words more inflection and meaning, so that your audience feels the emotion and power of the written words."

"Exactly. So now, play the same etude again and communicate your feelings through your horn. Speak through your horn. I had a great teacher say, *Play to someone you love, and make that love come through your horn as emotion.* If you do it well, that person will hear you, and so will the entire audience."

Dale played the etude several more times before moving to the two solos he would play in the concert. They discussed the songs' history and meaning, and finally how the solos should be interpreted.

"Let me show you, Dale. I think if you hear it, you will understand and be able to duplicate it." Mr. Schilke took a breath and played the solo from *Colonial Song*, which sent shivers up Dale's spine.

Colonial Song

"That was amazing! Look at the goosebumps on my arm."

"Excellent! That means I was able to convey a sense of emotion and expression through my playing. That is what you must strive for."

For the next twenty minutes, they took turns playing the solos, making adjustments as they went. As they finished the lesson, Mr. Jeffrey emerged from his office and commented on Dale's progress.

"Thanks, Mr. Jeffrey, but there's one more thing I want to do. I want to practice coming onstage from the band room. I want Mr. Schilke to demonstrate how a player focuses his thoughts when moving from a warm-up to a performance."

Mr. Jeffrey nodded. "The time from warm-up to performance is full of distractions. Getting yourself mentally prepared to perform is very important." Dale led Mr. Schilke to the band room, pointing to where the instruments were stored and the trophies on the back wall. Mr. Schilke smiled and said it reminded him of his younger days as a boy in Green Bay, Wisconsin.

On the drive back home, Dale's mind was so full of ideas and music that he found it hard to make conversation.

Sensing the boy's uneasiness, Mr. Schilke broke the silence. "I've put a lot of ideas about playing, listening, learning to focus, and dealing with adversity in your head today. I hope it's not too much for you. I don't expect you to understand it all right away; just apply what you can little by little."

Dale chose his words carefully as they pulled into the driveway. "I learned so much about playing today. But more important, I'm getting to know more about who I am and who I want to be." Dale opened the door to get out. "Thanks so much. I'll make you proud come Thursday's concert."

"Don't make me proud, make yourself proud."

Dale stood on the porch and watched Mr. Schilke's black Buick peel out of the driveway. Something caught his eye as he watched the car turn the corner on the next block. A shadowy figure walking a large dog was across the street by Chrissy's house. The person moved past the streetlight, and Dale realized it was Jim. Scout emerged from under the porch, emitting a low growl. The fur on the back of Scout's neck was raised as Jim and the large dog sauntered by. Dale bent down and patted Scout. "Good boy! I can always count on you to watch my back."

Chapter 18

HOLIDAY CONCERT

Dale sat on the stage by himself, imagining how he would sound before going to the band room to warm up. He surveyed the auditorium, the chairs and stands all in neat rows waiting to be filled by the band. Something, however, just didn't feel right about the set-up, but Dale couldn't put his finger on it.

As he stood to return to the band room, he saw it. For every stand, there should be two chairs. But the chairs looked different for some reason. He went to the end of the row and walked through the row, counting the chairs and matching two chairs for each stand. When he got to his seat, he had counted twenty-three chairs instead of the twenty-four there should have been.

"I must have miscounted." So he started recounting when Mr. Jeffrey walked onto the stage.

"Looks like you're taking some time to get a feel for the

auditorium tonight. I like to do the same thing."

"It helps me to calm down. But I think something's wrong with my row. I only count twenty-three chairs, not twenty-four."

"That can't be. Jim and Adrianne are in charge of set-up, and you know what sticklers they are for detail … but if you want, let me count."

Standing on the podium, Mr. Jeffrey counted. "You know, you're right. But where is the missing chair? There should be two per stand."

"Looks like it's where Jim and I sit. We only have one chair for our stand." While Mr. Jeffrey retrieved another chair, Dale thought: *So that was the plan … to distract me before my opening solo. How embarrassing it would have been not to have a chair! I wonder what else he has planned for tonight?*

Back in the band room, Mr. Jeffrey checked the flute section's intonation for the last time before the band went onstage. Jim had been particularly quiet during the rehearsals leading up to the concert, which bothered Dale. Neither boy acknowledged the other as they sat silently during the warm-up. Dale now focused his thoughts on his solos. He reminded himself that he was well prepared for the concert. Mentally, he fingered the parts and heard the melody in his head.

Mr. Jeffrey tapped his baton on the stand. "Let's settle down. I want you to relax and enjoy playing tonight. Remember, don't wave to your parents, and one last thing … do not sit down until the entire band has checked both their stands and chairs. If you are missing either one, raise your hand, and I'll get one to you before we all sit." Dale saw Adrianne turn in Jim's direction. Mr. Jeffrey saw the movement, and he focused his eyes on her. "Seems that Adrianne and Jim could have miscounted a chair, and I just want to make sure the set-up is correct." Adrianne, who was used to hearing only accolades, slumped in her chair. Turning to the first chair clarinet, Mr. Jeffrey said, "Lead us in, Rick."

The band filed out in rows toward the stage and began moving up the steps to the auditorium. Climbing the steps to the stage, the players were tightly packed in the narrow hallway, with little or no room to maneuver. The dim lights made it difficult to see. About halfway up the steps, the line suddenly stopped, causing the players to jam up, which made Dale bump into Jim. Dale saw Jim's elbow flex, so he quickly ducked, pretending to tie his shoe. Jim's elbow jutted back sharply. Instead of hitting Dale, the elbow clobbered Phil in the head.

"What the heck?" Phil cried, holding his head. "That almost hit me in the mouth!"

Jim turned to see Dale who was crouched down, smiling. Dale stood and rubbed Phil's head. "I think it looks fine; just a little red. Come on, we're moving again." The band entered each row in single file, and then standing quietly, the students checked to make sure they had both a chair and a stand. Dale looked out into the audience, and there in the front row was a tall dark-haired man sitting by himself. Dale thought, *That's odd, why would someone sit alone?*

Feeling a tap on his right arm, Dale looked up. Phil leaned over and said, "How's my head look?"

Dale took a quick look and said, "It looks good to me. Should be a great concert, don't you think, Phil?" Turning slightly toward Jim, Dale said, "Gee, I even have a chair! Fancy that!"

"Nice move, Kingston, but the concert isn't over yet," Jim said through gritted teeth.

Although Dale was acting confident on the outside, inside he repeated to himself: *There's no way he would sabotage his own concert. He can't do anything in front of all these people.* Dale's thoughts were interrupted when the audience applauded as Mr. Jeffrey entered the stage, bowed, and stepped on the podium. With a quick look at Dale, he gave the two pick-up beats just as Jim reached up and knocked the music on the floor.

Without hesitation, Dale played the opening solo to *Pepita Greus* perfectly, just as he had practiced a dozen times in the auditorium. Jim pretended it was an accident and picked up the music, frustrated that Dale had not been affected. When the march ended, Mr. Jeffrey pointed at Dale to stand and be recognized. When the applause died down, Dale leaned over to Jim and said, "Nice move, Petris, but next time remember Phil has the same part on his stand, so I didn't need our music."

Jim turned red with anger; he had run out of tricks. The remainder of the concert, including Dale's solo on *Colonial Song* was flawless. The final number was one of Dale's favorites, *A Christmas Festival* by Leroy Anderson. Because this was the first Christmas since the war ended, the holiday spirit filled the crowd. At the final cut-off, the band stood and bowed. Turning to the band, Mr. Jeffrey smiled and applauded the students. He then urged the audience to join the jazz band and combo in the cafeteria for some refreshments and music before the holiday break.

Before he left the stage, Dale noticed that the tall dark-haired man wrote something in a notebook before he left.

"Who's that guy?" he said as Sandra dragged him off the stage to the cafeteria for the reception.

Once the jazz band had set up, Dale saw Mr. Edwards sitting with his parents. They looked up to see Dale, who waved to them, much to Mr. Jeffrey's dissatisfaction. The opening number was *Sing, Sing, Sing* by Benny Goodman, featuring Dave on drum set followed by *In the Mood* by Glenn Miller, on which Dale had a huge solo. When it was time for the combo to play, the group moved to the front and played a new tune Mr. Edwards had played for them. They liked it so much they bought the music and learned it on their own. Mr. Jeffrey let Dale introduce the piece.

"We want to play a song we learned from a good friend of ours. Dizzy Gillespie and Charlie Parker first made this song famous. It's called *Groovin High*. This is for you, Mr.

Edwards." When they played the final chorus, Mr. Edwards was the first to shout, "Bravo."

Mr. Jeffrey returned to the mike to introduce the final number.

"This past summer you were introduced to Mr. Malone, a custodian at Emerson School who sang *Basin Street Blues* with the combo. Now we'd like him to join us again for our last number, *Minnie the Moocher* by Cab Calloway."

This song was one of the band's favorites. When the song ended, the crowd clapped and cheered. The students mingled with their parents and friends, enjoying the refreshments of punch and cookies. Dale's parents admitted that they were shocked to see the music fall off the stand, and they were very proud of the way Dale handled it.

Mr. Edwards was so pleased with the combo's performance of *Groovin High* that he shook each player's hand. When he got to Dale, he took an envelope out of his pocket.

"Here's an early Christmas present, Dale. I can't wait any longer to give it to you, especially after hearing your performance tonight. And by the way, your parents said it's OK."

Tearing the envelope open, Dale stared at the contents in disbelief. "Is this what I think it is? Are we really going to hear some live jazz?" Mr. Edwards laughed a deep laugh and said, "Live is better."

Chapter 19

CHICAGO

"Morning, Dale, where're you headed?" Mr. Paulson, the conductor, said as he stood at the door to the train.

"I'm going to Chicago to hear some jazz with Mr. Edwards today," he said, pointing down the platform at the man jogging towards them.

"So you aren't working?" Mr. Paulson asked, shaking Mr. Edwards's hand.

"Not today, but I do have to work both New Year's Eve and New Year's Day. That'll be one wild train ride, I'm sure."

Mr. Paulson chuckled. "Always is. Why don't you two go up to the second car? It's not very full, and you can stretch out before getting something to eat."

Dale climbed the steps to the train car, followed by Mr. Edwards. "Come on, Dale. Let's get out of this cold. I hope you brought some warm clothes. Chicago is one cold, windy city this time of year."

Dale pointed to the pack on his back. "I packed them in my backpack with my horn, like you suggested."

After storing their coats and Dale's backpack in the overhead bin, the pair settled into the large seats facing one another. After the conductor collected the tickets, the brakes hissed, and the train jerked forward, leaving Libertyville in the distance.

After hearing a rumbling from Dale's stomach, Mr. Edwards suggested a trip to the dining car. "It'll be fun to be waited on and let someone else cook for a change."

They got the royal treatment during breakfast, with all of Mr. Edwards's co-workers stopping at the table and providing extra-special service. After getting their coffee, Dale took a sip and leaned back, enjoying the smooth ride and the sound from the rails beneath the train.

"So how'd you get to know all of these great jazz players in Chicago?"

"Well, it started when I went to work on the Illinois Central Railroad that ran between New Orleans and Chicago. When I first started, I was a red cap and loaded luggage. Then, I worked my way into the dining car, first as a bus boy, and then as a server. The cooks were so nice to me—they taught me the basics of food preparation. Eventually, I turned into a chef on that same train, the *City of New Orleans*.

Dale crinkled his forehead. "I don't understand how that's related to Chicago jazz." Mr. Edwards grinned, and took a bite of his steaming scrambled eggs that had just arrived.

"Well, they called it the Great Migration. In the South, there was little work during the Depression in the 1930s, especially for black folks like me. I was lucky to get a job with the railroad, but many others were out of work. In the North, and particularly Chicago, there were good wages for factory work and also for musicians. The musicians went to Chicago in droves. I would load their luggage, which provided an opportunity for me to get to know them. When I moved into the dining car, I got to know even more musicians. Some of the players were so poor that I would slip them food—maybe a roll and a slice of ham, which they really appreciated. Gradually, they would tell me where they were playing, and on my layovers, I would visit the clubs on Chicago's South Side ... and I fell in love with live jazz."

"What's a layover?"

"When you worked on a train that runs from New Orleans to Chicago, it takes so long that when you get to Chicago, you had worked more than the usual number of hours. So you had to rest up before going back. That was called a layover, and usually it was twenty-four to thirty-six hours, which gave me plenty of time to go to the clubs."

"Wait, you didn't sleep?"

"I was young and full of life. Why sleep when you could go out in the greatest town in the world and hear jazz? Sleep was second to music at that time in my life. I knew all the players by name, and I would listen to their music regularly. I made a lot of great friends. But then the war came, and I was assigned to fight in the 92nd Infantry Division, an all-black division known as the Buffalo Division. That kept me from going to hear jazz in Chicago until I came home last year. Now I go every chance I get."

"You fought in the 92nd division of the Army?" Dale looked at Mr. Edwards with amazement.

"I sure did. We distinguished ourselves and began to break down the barriers of discrimination, although we have a long way to go. I lost a lot of great friends fighting in Italy. Do you know where we got the nickname *Buffalo Soldier* from?"

Dale shook his head.

"It came from the American Indians back in the 1860s who saw the voluntary black cavalry soldiers. They called them Buffalo Soldiers or 'black white men' out of respect for a worthy enemy. I'll have to show you our division patch. It's a circular shoulder patch featuring a black buffalo on a drab olive-colored background."

Dale hoped he could see it some time, and Mr. Edwards promised he would.

"Let me explain how all this fits into what we're doing today. After hearing you practice and attending the concert, I wanted to expose you to live jazz. I called several friends of mine who play at a club and asked if I could bring you to listen and also play in a session. They suggested we come up today on the twenty-eighth of December because they're not very busy and would be practicing for the big New Year's Eve party coming up."

Dale hesitated a moment before admitting, "I'm a little nervous about going to this area of the city."

"Don't worry. More and more white musicians are going to the South Side to listen and learn from these great players. I know where to go, and if you're with me, you'll be fine. I think you'll enjoy meeting and playing with these jazz greats."

"Aren't we going to a club where adults are? Do they let kids in?"

"It's technically a night club, but during the afternoon, the club is closed so the musicians can practice. I arranged for you to play the first set in the evening, which is usually a smaller crowd. The second and third sets get crowded, but we'll be on our way home by then. Just relax and have a good time—this will be a trip of a lifetime."

Mr. Edwards thanked his friends for the great food and service. They made their way down the swaying aisle to their seats, putting their feet up and falling fast asleep.

Dale awoke as he felt the train slowing. He looked out the window and saw that they were rounding the curve toward Union Station. The familiar tall buildings reminded him of his trip to Ravinia last summer. This time, however, snowflakes were falling from the low gray clouds that enveloped the buildings.

"Some lake-effect snow, so don't be worried."

"Lake-effect, what's that?" Dale asked, watching the large flakes float by the train window.

"That's when the lake water is warmer than the air. When the wind blows toward the city, it picks up moisture from the lake, and if the temperature is right, it causes lake-effect snow. It's not like a regular storm that usually comes from the north or west."

"It sure is pretty, but it looks cold out there." Dale put on his jacket and warm gloves, and lifted his backpack from the upper compartment. "How do we get to the club?"

"Easy, we take the bus." Dale and Mr. Edwards thanked the conductor and followed the crowd into Union Station. Climbing the stairs to the outside, they waited at a stop for the bus.

During the ride, Mr. Edwards pointed out the different buildings and told the history of the city and where they were going. They had to transfer to a different bus, but Dale felt confident under the guidance of Mr. Edwards.

"When we get to the club, stay close and follow my lead. Take a deep breath, and get ready for an experience few your age ever get to have. Ready?"

The bus jerked to a stop outside a two-story brick building with the name Club Delisa over the door.

"I'm ready, so lead the way."

The doors opened and the bus emptied, with people dispersing in different directions. Dale and Mr. Edwards went inside the dimly lit club entrance. The smell of smoke still lingered in the air. As they made their way down the narrow hallway to the back, they could hear musicians warming up and practicing songs for the night's session.

"Deep breath, you're doing fine," Mr. Edwards said, leading Dale to a table where a man with coffee-colored skin sat. A cornet with a worn finish lay on the table.

"Hey, Chuck, is that you? Come on over here, man."

"Who's Chuck?" Dale blurted out before realizing the man was talking to Mr. Edwards.

Mr. Edwards leaned over and whispered, "When we're in the club, I'm Chuck. Calling me Mr. Edwards is not cool in here."

Chuck shook the man's hand heartily and introduced his young companion to Jesse Miller. "Great to meet a budding jazz cornet player." He looked Dale up and down. "Not many of your kind get down here."

Dale extended his hand. "Nice to meet you, Mr. Miller."

"Sorry, boy, there are no misters in here. Please call me Jesse. We jazz lovers are all one."

"OK, Jesse, glad to meet you."

Moving onto the stage, the members of the band greeted Dale warmly. They offered him a chair and invited him to listen to the changes they were making to several songs. Dale knew what changes were and was able to hear most of the major chords, but with some of the minor chords, he wasn't sure.

Dale leaned over to Chuck. "I hear most of the changes, but I'm not familiar with some of the chords."

Chuck gladly explained. "They're using substitutions, which are other chords that fit the melody and that give the song more interest and variety. You'll notice they change the chords during the solos, which allows the soloist to explore the melody in more interesting and colorful ways."

"I don't know if I can follow that yet."

"Don't worry ... they'll keep it pretty straight until you feel comfortable. Then they'll begin to push your ear and soloing skills. Sit back and just listen. Don't overthink what they're doing. Breathe in the music so it becomes part of your soul," Chuck said, taking a deep breath, as if he were inhaling all the notes in the room.

Dale sat back and listened, admiring the ways the soloist, piano, bass, and drummer interacted with one another. Jazz was the ultimate team sport with each person having to read the others' minds, musical expressions, and rhythms, responding to and encouraging the soloist to take greater risks. After several numbers, the group took a break, and Jesse came over.

"What do you think?"

Dale couldn't contain his enthusiasm. "You make the music sound so easy when it isn't. And the way you relate to each other and communicate is beyond words."

Jesse glanced at Chuck and winked. "That's a lot of words. How about just one word to answer my question?"

Dale blushed, not understanding, until he saw Jesse and Chuck smile. Then he knew they were kidding him.

"Cool," Dale said, smiling back.

"That's better. Now remember that when you play. It's not about how many notes you play; it's what you *say* with the ones you play. Sometimes less is better."

At that moment, Dale realized his training had begun, and he was invited onstage to join the group. For the next hour and a half, the players worked the two pieces Dale would play, *Groovin High* and *Lester Leaps In.* When Dale's lip was about worn out from playing, they stopped and sat around talking.

"Man, you've got a good ear. I like a cat that listens to what we say, and then does it. You play more like a black person than a white one. Chuck, I think you've had him listening to some Led Belly, Lester Young, and Dizzy Gillespie from how he plays."

"How did you know that I listened to those players?"

"When a man plays, his past teachers and experiences can always be heard. Chuck, why don't you take Dale to Gladys's Luncheonette for some real food before the first set? She'll be glad to see ya. You got about two hours."

Dale and Chuck sat on the bus talking about what he had learned in the rehearsal and how good the players were. The bus stopped across the street from Gladys's Luncheonette.

"This is the finest soul food place in the south of Chicago. This place will put your grandmother's cooking to shame,"

Chuck guaranteed. As they entered the luncheonette, a short, dark-skinned woman wearing an apron met them. She had spotted Chuck from across the street, and immediately gave him a big hug.

"I haven't seen you since you went off to war. And, from the looks of it, you survived with all your parts still intact." She patted his belly and said, "Although you do look a might skinny for my tastes!" Then she noticed Dale standing silently in Chuck's shadow.

"This boy with you?"

"Sure is. Dale, I want you to meet the best cook in town, Gladys Holcomb, the owner of this fine establishment."

Looking Dale over, she paused, "Well, any friend of Chuck's is a friend of mind. Get over here and give old Gladys a hug."

Seeing the smile on her face made Dale relax. "Nice to meet you, Ma'am."

"My, you're a polite one," and she whisked them to a booth with deep leather cushions.

Dale had never tasted such food before! He started with smothered chicken, collard greens, and cornbread, followed by a peach cobbler that melted in his mouth. Dale put his head against the back of the booth, patting his stomach just as Gladys slid next to him.

"From the looks of your stomach, I think you're about to blow up. Tell me, what is a boy like you doing with Chuck down here?"

For the next several minutes they talked about jazz, blues, swing, and how Chuck and Dale came to know each other.

"You mean you're playing tonight with Jesse Miller at Club Delisa? You must be one special person to play with those cats. I might have to close up early and come hear you myself." Just as fast as she slid in, she slipped out of the booth to wait on another customer.

Chuck gathered his coat and stood. "We don't want to miss the next bus in this cold. I hope you can play tonight after all that food."

"Stuffed I am, but not so much that I can't play."

Chuck left a generous tip, and they hopped the next bus. When they arrived, they went in the back door and met Jesse.

"Before you warm up, you need a nickname, Dale. Jazz players never use their given name. They always add something like Slim, Fats, or Red. Think about it and let me know before I introduce you to the crowd. And, I do mean crowd ... looks like we're in for a busy night."

Dale looked wide-eyed at Chuck. He had been ready to play for a half-deserted room. Chuck patted him confidently on the back and led him to a back room. Dale got his horn out and played some long tones, trying to come up with an appropriate jazzy sounding nickname.

Jesse poked his head in the door. "The band's going out. Sit here and enjoy. At the end of the set, we'll have you sit in and play the two songs you learned today. Have fun jamming with us!" Jesse was about to leave when he stopped suddenly. "Hey, I almost forgot. What's your nickname?"

"Catfish," Dale said. "Dale "Catfish" Kingston."

"Cool!" and Jesse turned and walk onstage to the applause and cheers of the crowd.

The group played for about thirty-five minutes before Dale saw Jesse point at him backstage and mouth the words, "You're next."

Dale took a deep breath, trying to remember all they had taught him.

"Now welcome to the stage a young jazz player who's probably scared to death. Please give a warm Club welcome to Dale "Catfish" Kingston."

The applause started, but when Dale stepped onstage, it dropped off. As he looked into the bright lights, he could only see the silhouettes of the audience who were talking and pointing in his direction. A few people laughed and stood up. Dale could see Chuck, sitting proudly at a front table, nodding his head in encouragement, which reminded him to stay relaxed and enjoy the opportunity of playing with these great musicians.

"Ah one, ah two, ah one, two, three," and the song started with a short piano introduction. Dale watched the sax player who was the soloist before his solo. They told him when the player finished, he would nod for Dale to start. Focusing on his entrance helped Dale take his mind off the people watching him.

Dale raised his horn and played a simple short phrase. Little by little, he developed the musical idea both rhythmically and melodically, building to a high C that he held as long as he could, nodding off to the band, which joined him for the final head and chorus. When his solo ended, the crowd erupted and whistled their approval.

Jesse quieted the audience and announced the last song of the set, *Lester Leaps In*. He counted the song off, and this time it went even better than before, ending with the soloist trading eights and fours before playing the head. Dale hadn't expected the other soloist to respond to his playing, and this unexpected response was the thrill of a lifetime. When the final number ended, the band took a break backstage. Chuck joined them, his eyes gleaming.

"Chuck, you're right ... he's great."

Dale looked at Chuck and said seriously, "Wait, Jesse, that's a lot of words, don't you think?" At first, Jesse furrowed his brow, but when Dale broke into a smile, he said, "Cool. I think that sums it up."

The other members of the band slapped Dale on the back, congratulating him on his fine jazz debut.

When the group started the second set, Dale and Chuck walked out into the cold night air. The lake-effect snow flurries were swirling in the air.

"Chuck, this was the best Christmas present I've ever had. I'll never forget it."

"Cool!" said Chuck as they ran to catch the bus that was pulling up to take them to the train and finally home.

Chapter 20

Marching Orders

The band room was abuzz the first school day after the holidays. Students shared stories of sledding in Simpson Park, presents they received, and trips to faraway relatives' homes. Hundreds of conversations seemed to be going on at once. Dale overheard Chrissy describing to Victor her first hunt. She twirled around, showing off the pheasant feather that was stuck in her ponytail. Bridget gently stroked Bobby's cheek, the fading remnants of a black eye from the snowball fight at the fort still evident. Other students wore new sweaters or woolen shirts, but the loudest conversations were around the blackboard in the front of the room. Dale wondered what the commotion was about as he took his cornet out of the case.

Adrianne rushed up to him and pulled him by the arm toward the blackboard. "Look at the contest assignments! You have to see where Mr. Jeffrey has assigned each student for the state contest. This is the most exciting part of the year," Adrianne squealed, pushing her way through the crowd with a bewildered Dale in tow.

"You'll see," she said, nudging the last few students out of the way. "Look, he has two columns—one for the solos and one for ensembles. See my name at the top of the solo list?" her fingernail tapping emphatically on the board. "That means I am the top flute player representing the flute section at state." Then she pointed to Chrissy's name below hers. "That means if I can't perform or do not prepare my solo up to Mr. Jeffrey's standards, then Chrissy is next in line to take my spot." With that, Adrianne whirled around, nearly knocking P.J. off his feet while he was standing on his tiptoes directly behind her.

"I've waited my whole life for a chance to beat West Liberty Junior High," she sighed, "and now my dream has come true!"

Adrianne left Dale standing in front of the board as she dashed over to some other girls in the flute section and gave them a hug. Then Dale felt a shove in his back.

"Well, hotshot! Looks like you're still number two. Don't think that fancy private teacher can help you beat me this time," Jim taunted, giving Dale one last shove before moving back in the crowd.

Dale didn't turn around or react to Jim's comments or shove. He remained motionless, staring at the list of names. He felt another shove that was followed by an arm around his shoulder.

"Do you believe we're the number one brass ensemble over the eighth graders?" Karl shouted over the crowd.

Dale searched the board, but couldn't find the list of ensembles.

Just then the lights flicked on and off. In a loud voice, Mr. Jeffrey said, "Let's take our seats and begin rehearsal. I have a lot of material to cover today." He waded into the crowd at the board, shooing students to their seats.

"Mr. Jeffrey will explain it. Come on, we don't want to be the last ones standing," Victor said, zigzagging through the chairs to take his seat.

It took several minutes and Mr. Jeffrey having to use his loud voice, but finally the band settled down and played Bach's chorale, *Wach auf, mein Herz,* which meant *Wake Up, My Heart*. Dale felt good about playing again after the long vacation and all the fun he had with his friends. At the end of the chorale, the director instructed the students to remain quiet and calm and not ask questions until he was finished.

"I'm sure the seventh graders are a little overwhelmed by the excitement this morning. I would be, too. For the first time in ten years, we have the quality of players to win our first state contest and defeat West Liberty Junior High." Forgetting the original instructions, the band clapped and cheered. P.J. stood up, cupped his hands, and did a perfect imitation of Principal Hamilton's lion ROOOOOOAAAAAAAAAAR. Mr. Jeffrey suppressed a slight smile and held up his hand for silence.

"Don't get too excited. We have eight weeks of hard work getting ready for contest on Friday, March 1st. We also will be preparing for our next concert on March 22nd, the last day of school before spring break."

Mr. Jeffrey then explained the contest procedures. "Each student has been placed in a category that will earn us the most points possible."

"I can enter one player from each section in the solo categories and eight ensembles total from the entire band." He then droned on about the need for a backup, but Dale had already heard this from Adrianne. His mind drifted to thoughts of vacation, when he felt a pencil bounce off his foot. He looked over to see Sandra nodding her head toward the podium. Mr. Jeffrey was looking directly at him. "Are you listening, young man?"

"Sorry, Mr. Jeffrey," Dale said. He heard a low snicker to his left, which he ignored.

"As I was saying, I've put the quintet with Dale, Sandra, Victor, Karl, and P.J. as our number one brass ensemble event. They're the one group that we need more than any other group to get a Division I at contest. In the past, we've been able to match West Liberty for every event. Last year, we tied. As you eighth graders recall, in the event of a tie, the directors can select one ensemble that had received a Division I earlier in the day to play a tie breaker for a panel of judges in the auditorium as all the schools watch. Winner takes all. Last year, the brass quintet of Jim, Phil, Mike, Pete, and Joe lost by just two points. If Dale's group can get a Division I in the first round, and each soloist and ensemble can match scores with West's scores, then we would have a chance to be in the tie breaker." Mr. Jeffrey's voice grew more forceful, and he punctuated his words by tapping his baton on the stand.

"This year, I'm investing in Dale's group, although seventh graders, to break that tie. The eighth-grade ensemble will be the backup. West won't expect us to have a group they've never seen play the final tie breaker." His eyes darted back and forth, his words *crescendoing* into a finale. "This year, East will win state and reclaim the trophy that is rightfully ours!"

For the rest of the rehearsal, the band sight-read through several pieces, but Dale's mind was on what Mr. Jeffrey had said. *Jim's group was number two because they lost last year.* Dale was confused ... wasn't there already enough tension between him and Jim without Mr. Jeffrey seeming to fan the flames of their feud? Is this the way Mr. Jeffrey motivated students, or was it by accident that they seemed to be competing against one another instead of working together? At the end of rehearsal, Mr. Jeffrey excused the band.

Jim leaned over as Dale closed the music folder. "Hey, hotshot! Don't think our brass ensemble isn't going to work our tails off to beat you for the top spot."

Dale had a choice of how to respond. Say nothing or say something; he chose the wrong one. Standing up, he leaned down into Jim's face and whispered, "First, Jim, I didn't know you and your ensemble had tails. Second, I think your tails were between your legs after losing last time. Lastly, if I were you, I'd be more worried about your solo and yourself for a change. I think you'll mess up because you're a screwup." As he walked away, he muttered, "You're your own worst enemy."

As he uttered the last word, Dale realized he had done the wrong thing. Instead of walking away, he had escalated the problem, not solved it. His thoughts were interrupted by the brass ensemble running up to him, excited about being named the number one ensemble and having the opportunity to play on such a high level.

"Dale, how come you aren't excited? This is what we have worked for, isn't it?" P.J. asked.

Dale hesitated. "I'm not sure what to think. But yes, I'm excited." While his friends continued to celebrate, Dale removed himself from the group and put away his horn. The bell rang, and he walked by himself to his next class, thinking ... *the way I reacted to Jim makes me wonder if I'm the one who's turning into a bully.*

Chapter 21

Rivalry Begins

Pete, Mike, Joe, Victor, and Dale sat on the gym floor, catching their breath after the last practice before the final game of the year. East Libertyville would play West Libertyville for the conference championship. The rest of the team had gone to the locker room, but Pete, Mike, and Joe asked Dale and Victor to stay behind.

Pete, the team captain, wiped the sweat from his face. "We asked you to stay because we believe that you two have done a great job this season coming off the bench. You've never disappointed us the entire season. I think I can speak for Mike and Joe and say that when we first met you on the steps of the junior high when you came for your audition last spring, we thought you would be arrogant and self-centered. Jim encouraged us to pick on you, but now that we've played with you on the team and in band, I think we were wrong."

Dale's breathing began to even out as Pete's words began to sink in.

"I understand that you don't trust us after the way we treated you earlier, but we want you to know that is over."

Mike interrupted and said, "The three of us talked and felt that before the big game, you needed to know that the bullying is over. We want to move on. This game is about team building, but not just in basketball. Three of the boys on West's team are in band and were the ones who played against us in the tie breaker last year. Mr. Jeffrey didn't tell you seventh graders the whole story about how we lost."

Dale glanced at Victor, who spoke up. "I don't understand. Why would Mr. Jeffrey not tell the whole story? He made it sound like you blew it and should have won."

"I'll take it from here," Joe said, "but you can't say anything to anyone about this. How we saw the tie breaker and how Mr. Jeffrey saw it were not the same. When the contest was tied, Mr. Jeffrey called the band together to discuss what group would play the finals. Our brass quintet was the number two brass group, and we were excited to have helped get the band to the finals by getting a Division I. The top groups he should have picked were eighth graders: a flute quartet, a French horn quartet, or a brass quintet. These groups were really good, much better than us."

Pete continued the story. "To make a long story short, Mr. Jeffrey went back and forth about who should play, causing a lot of anxiety to build up in the players. Just as he was going to announce his decision, one of the other directors came in and told him who West was going to use—a brass quintet of seventh graders, hoping the judges would be swayed by a younger group playing against an older group. So then, out of the blue, he picks us with only fifteen minutes left to warm up!

But, here is the part he doesn't know and didn't tell. Once he announced our group, he left the room to take the band to the auditorium. Well, the eighth graders he didn't pick were really upset and stayed back and started hassling us. They taunted us, saying, 'No way you're better than us,' and 'You'd better win,' and just a lot of negative talk as they left the room. I still remember the five of us sitting in the warm-up room by ourselves. We were so nervous feeling the pressure that I almost threw up. You know the rest of the story: we went out and lost. I don't think West was better ... we just felt so much peer pressure from the eighth graders and Mr. Jeffrey, we clutched."

Dale began to understand why he felt the tension of competition with Jim. "So is that why there seems to be so much tension and competition for chairs, solos, and contest? Is Mr. Jeffrey trying to motivate us to work harder through competition?"

This time Pete didn't answer, but Mike stepped in. "In a way, yes. There seems to be a lot of intimidation and competition between the seventh and eighth grades. I also think there is competition between individuals in the same grade. I don't think Mr. Jeffrey is doing it on purpose, but there's definitely a desire to win at all costs."

"That would explain why Jim is so pushy and intimidates us," Dale replied.

"I'm not sure what Jim's problem is, but I want you to know, we are done with Jim's actions. We'll play in his ensemble, but we're not going to be a part of bullying you anymore. We want you to have the chance to prove yourself without being hassled by us," Joe added.

Dale and Victor responded by leaning over and shaking the three boys' hands.

Pete's voice got serious. "We're not done yet. I want us to take this game with West and use it to learn how to play hard, but without the pressure. Remember that the three best players on West's team are also the same ones from the quintet we lost to last year. I'm sure they'll badger us about losing the contest, hoping to distract us and make us mad so we mess up. If we can keep calm and not let it affect our game, we can win. In addition, we'll be able to help you guys learn how to handle this big game with no pressure from us. Then maybe you can apply what you learn during this game to the contest and not repeat what happened to us."

"It's a deal. Now that we've talked, I feel like we're a team, not only on the basketball floor, but also in band," Dale said.

Pete stood up and the rest of the boys followed his lead. "Let's practice a few of the plays we've learned and also a couple of new ones we think might work. Mr. Cabutti will put you two in at the end because West doesn't know you and will have no idea about what you can do. I think he'll put the five of us in together, and we'll have to rise to the challenge."

Victor raised his arm in the air. "All for one, and one for all!"

The other boys lifted theirs, and their arms formed a cone above their heads. "All for one, and one for all!"

For the next hour, the five boys worked on old and new plays, working out possible scenarios that West might use against them. Just as they were walking off the court, Mr. Cabutti came out of the locker room.

"Hey, practice was done an hour ago. What are you doing out here?"

Pete stepped forward out of breath. "You told us to lead by example, so that's what we're doing. Dale and Victor have really improved, and we wanted to make sure they felt good about the plays and how we believe in them."

"Pete, that's why you're captain," Mr. Cabutti said, patting him on the back. "OK, hit the showers. I'll see you at the game tomorrow. Oh, one last thing," he said putting his hand in the air, "All for one, and one for all!" Chuckling, he walked back to his office.

As the boys headed to the locker room, Pete lingered so he could walk with Dale. "I don't know how to say this, so I'll give it to you straight. Watch your back with Jim. Since we've broken ties with him, he really seems angry. Just as a warning, he's gotten a big new dog that seems mean. I don't know why he got a dog, but I do remember your dog chasing us up a tree and tearing off his pocket." Pete swung the door open for Dale. "It's probably nothing, but just be careful."

Chapter 22

OFF THE BENCH

Dale and his dad finished their workout and sat on the mattresses. Scout was sprawled on the landing of the stairs leading to the kitchen sleeping.

"Do you think we can take Scout to the vet? He just doesn't seem like himself. He doesn't want to go outside, and all he wants to do is sleep."

"I agree he does seem to be slowing down. We could take him in on Saturday."

Dale appreciated his dad's understanding. "Thanks, that will help me focus on the big game."

"I wish I didn't have to work. I'd love to see you play. Do you think you'll get in the game?"

"I'm not sure, but Pete, the captain, thinks we may get in at the end."

Dad thoughtfully stroked his chin. "Sometimes coming off the bench is tough since you tend to be cold and not warmed up."

Dale brightened, "When I had my last lesson with Mr. Schilke, we talked about symphony players having to sit for a long time and then performing at a high level. That's kind of like coming off the bench. He told me that it's all mental, that you have no control over what other people say or do. You only have control over how you react to them."

"He's right. In the war, we were trained to stay cool under fire. Don't let your emotions get in your way. Be proactive, not reactive if possible."

"It's funny that we can learn the same things from different activities."

"No, not really, because lessons learned in one situation can be applied in others," Dad said as he stood up, and the two headed upstairs.

After a hearty breakfast, Dale grabbed his backpack and jacket for the walk to school with his friends in the cold February morning. His head was clear, and he felt relaxed about the game that night. The music contest was still four weeks away, and both his solo and the brass quintet's practices were going well.

When Dale, Chrissy, and Victor arrived at school, the halls were lined with banners proclaiming Lion Pride, and yellow and black streamers hung from the ceiling. The cheerleaders had even decorated the team's lockers with the players' names and jersey numbers.

Sandra ran up to the trio. "What do you think? Do you like it? Chrissy, Bridget, and I helped the pep club decorate last night after your practice. We thought you would never leave the gym. What were you talking to Pete, Joe, and Mike about? It looked kind of serious."

"Nothing really. They just wanted to talk about the game and work out some possible plays. They're really nice guys," Dale said. Dale lowered his voice and looked around before he spoke. "Pete also told me that they'd had enough of the bullying."

"About time! Now Jim is all by himself, which, I am sure, he won't like." Sandra grabbed Dale's arm. "Come on. Enough of that *Jim* talk! I want to show you this *gym* before we go to band," she said, dragging Dale and Victor down the decorated hall.

The rest of the day flew by, with students and teachers wishing the team good luck. Mr. Cabutti hosted a team meal in the cafeteria before the game, making the boys feel very special.

After the meal, the boys dressed in their home uniforms that were gold with black trim. The team was anxious, causing the players to fidget on the benches in the locker room. They could hear the muffled cheering of the crowd. The team became quiet and focused. Mr. Cabutti had already given his pre-game speech during dinner, and now it was just the boys sitting together, waiting for the championship game to begin.

Pete stood and faced the team. "I want you to look into each other's eyes," he began. "I want you to see the commitment, dedication, and trust in each other we have established over the last ten weeks." Looking at Dale and Victor he added, "I also see good friends and people I believe in. I see no fear, no doubt. I know when this game gets tough, we'll focus our thoughts, calm our fellow players, and execute, execute, execute. Don't think, just react, and play with heart and commitment. Read each other's eyes and thoughts, and let's play as one. Remember, we are lions and should be feared by those we are about to play!"

The boys didn't cheer but instead put their hands into the circle, shouting in unison "Roooоaaaaaaar to success" before running out into the standing-room-only gym to screams and cheers.

After the warm-up and before the team introductions, Pete pointed out the three players from West's brass quintet. They were tall and fast, but they didn't look very muscular, which Dale thought he might be able to use to his advantage. Dale looked up at the home stands, seeing his friends sitting together in one section, waving and yelling at him. He also found Jim in the crowd, sitting in the first row behind the basket, directly in a free-throw shooter's line of sight. Intuitively, Dale knew he wouldn't be cheering for him or Victor.

The referee threw up the opening jump ball. From the onset, the teams were evenly matched. At the end of the first half, East was down two points, but several of the players had three or four fouls. Mr. Cabutti stomped back into the locker room.

"I'm not very happy with the number of fouls. The refs seem to be calling fouls for minor contact on us but not on West. If that's the way this game is going, we'll still have to keep playing physical, but we need to be smarter. If we can stay within two to four points going into the fourth quarter, West will begin to tire. I want to keep up the fast-break offense and play man-to-man defense this next half. When we go out for warm-ups, Dale, be sure you and Victor practice your free throws. I may need to put you in if we get in more foul trouble."

Mr. Cabutti looked at his two young players. "Are you feeling up to this?"

Dale stepped forward. "Victor and I are ready. We'll do whatever the team needs."

Mr. Cabutti bent down and motioned for the team to huddle up. "All hands in. Who are we?"

The team chanted in unison. "We are lions! Rooooaaaaaaar to success!" Then they ran out of the locker room to the cheers of a ramped-up crowd for the second-half warm-up.

The teams had switched ends of the court, and Jim was now on the side East used for the warm-up. Dale stood at the goal line and released a shot toward the basket, but each time he got ready, Jim would wave his arms behind the basket. It worked. Dale's first three practice shots weren't even close. Pete saw what was happening and stepped in front of Jim for Dale's last two practice shots. Both went in. Pete turned toward Jim and said something, causing Jim to laugh.

Disgusted, Pete returned to Dale and said, "Listen ... focus on your shots, not on Jim or anyone else. We're going to need you." He patted him on the back, adding, "It's time to step up."

At the sound of the buzzer, Dale grimly threw one last ball that bounced off the rim before he trotted over to the bench for the start of the third quarter.

Before the referee ran out to center court, Dale could overhear some of the West players taunting Pete, "Once a loser, always a loser." Then after Mike missed a free throw, they muttered sarcastically, "Nice shot! Still can't handle the pressure." Each time they got a chance, West players made sure to push or shove when the referees were not looking.

Finally, halfway through the fourth quarter, Rick, who was the co-captain, couldn't take it any longer. He shoved a West player, only to get a technical and foul out. Mr. Cabuttii jumped off the bench, resulting in another technical. The crowd screamed as the tension between the two teams grew. After West made both shots, Mr. Cabutti quickly pulled the team together. "Rick is out. Dale, you're in, and Victor will go in for Billy. I want to send a message that we're not going to take any more cheap shots. Stay physical. Dale, you and Victor have no fouls, so play hard. Take a charge or two, but jam the lane and don't let up on the man-to-man. We have two minutes left and are down by three. 'Pass, pass, pass.' Alright, all in!"

As the boys walked out on the floor, Pete whispered, "Be ready. I have a feeling they'll pass to whoever is guarding you."

West had the ball. As the players lined up for the inbound pass, one of the three shoved Dale in the back, whispering, "Fresh meat—I smell fear." The player moved quickly behind Dale. "You're that hotshot cornet player. I think you'll clutch just like your friends did last year at contest."

Dale didn't answer. He made sure his arms were out and his feet were planted firmly on the ground. He knew they would pass toward whomever Dale was guarding. The whistle blew, and as the players jostled for position, Dale realized he could use his weight and strength to block the West player. He felt the player begin to push off and go for the ball, so Dale dropped his shoulder into the player's chest, pushed back and quickly spun around, causing the player to fall to the floor as the ball was passed in. Dale caught the ball, and Pete, anticipating Dale's move, headed down the court unguarded. Dale lobbed the ball, and Pete in full stride caught the ball and made an easy lay-up. The East crowd jumped to their feet.

Dale turned to the fallen player, put out his hand and pulled him up and close.

"So, is that what fear smells like? And yes, I am that hotshot cornet player. Game on."

For the next minute, both teams traded baskets with East still behind by two. With fifteen seconds left in the game, West got the ball and charged down the court with the player Dale was guarding catching a pass and driving for the basket. West had a two-point advantage.

Dale heard Mr. Cabutti's voice in his head. "If you have to take a charge, take it. Jam the lane."

Dale stepped in, squared his shoulders, and let the West player run into him, taking a big hit and sending him to the floor. The ref called the West player for charging, giving Dale a chance to shoot two free throws. As they walked back to the foul line, Pete reminded Dale.

"Stay cool. You get two shots. Make the first one, and don't worry about the second one. Mike or Joe will get the rebound on the second one for sure. We've got them spooked."

Dale agreed. "Remember, if I miss, I always miss to the right."

Dale stepped to the line as the crowd from West screamed, hoping to rattle Dale. Jim was under the basket, yelling, but Dale couldn't hear what he was saying because of the noise. He'd practiced shooting free throws quickly by taking two quick bounces and then shooting. Taking too much time would cause more tension. Dale bounced the ball twice and released it. A huge roar rose from the East fans as the ball swished through the basket. On the second shot, he repeated the process, but as he shot, Jim jumped out of his seat, faking excitement and causing Dale to miss. The basketball went wide right. Joe, anticipating the shot, was in the air grabbing the ball, pulling it tightly to his chest. The West players tried to wrestle it from him. With just ten seconds left, Mr. Cabutti called time out.

"We've got the ball. There's time for one play. If we score, we will win." Mr. Cabutti drew a play on a small chalkboard and gave each player his assignment. As the team returned to the court, Pete gathered them together.

"I don't like the play. If we run Cabutti's play, West will stop us. Remember the play we practiced yesterday by ourselves? Let's run it. If I'm wrong, and we lose, I'll take the blame."

Dale quickly stepped out of bounds, and the referee tossed him the ball. Mr. Cabutti sputtered, "That's not the play! Pete is supposed to inbound the ball!" The boys paid no attention. Dale held the ball for a second, not moving, and then he and the other boys raised their arms into the air in unison and yelled, "All for one, and one for all!" causing the West players to look up, giving Victor just enough time to slip away from the boy guarding him and head for the basket.

With one hand, Dale passed the ball through the legs of Pete, who faked trying to get it, which allowed the ball to bounce into the waiting hands of Victor. He turned and dribbled the ball once before making an easy lay-up as the buzzer blared, ending the game. West's players were stunned as the students ran onto the floor, lifting Victor onto the shoulders of an eighth grader. Pete ran over to Dale and gave him a big hug.

"Great pass, Kingston. Time to celebrate, but I think someone wants to talk to us first." Pete motioned toward Mr. Cabutti, who was working his way through the crowd toward Dale and Pete.

"All for one, and one for all? You didn't run the play I called. What is that about, Pete?"

Pete looked sheepishly at his coach. "We knew they would expect the final shot to be taken by Joe, Mike, or me, so we worked a play out yesterday after practice that would confuse them."

"It not only confused them, but it also confused me. I almost had a heart attack!" Mr. Cabutti's face then broke into a wide smile as he clutched his chest.

"Sorry, coach, but we knew they'd never guard Victor or expect him to get the ball. We figured they hadn't seen Dale do a one-handed bounce pass. With me faking to get the ball, they would be looking at me and the ball, allowing Victor to get free."

"But what was the 'All for one, and one for all' about?"

"It was a way to disrupt their play. By raising our arms and yelling, they were distracted just enough." Mr. Cabutti shook his head at the ingenuity of his players. To the delight of the East students, Pete and Dale and their teammates shouted, "All for one, and one for all!" before the student body engulfed the team.

The celebration lasted about thirty minutes before the team was able to head to the locker room. As they picked up some clean towels on their way to their lockers, the realization of the win hit both Dale and Victor.

Now their focus would shift to winning the state music contest.

Chapter 23

SCOUT

"That must have been an exciting game yesterday. I went to East and never liked West," Mr. Coogan, the veterinarian, said after listening to Scout's chest with a stethoscope.

Dale carefully watched as the vet opened Scout's mouth and examined his teeth. "Is something wrong with Scout?" Dale asked expectantly.

"Scout's only eight years old, but last year was really hard on him. Being outside most of the winter and traveling all the way to Montana took its toll. His heart doesn't sound as strong as it should for a dog his age. You might want to take care so he doesn't exert himself too much."

Dale hugged Scout, holding back his tears so his dad wouldn't see.

"Dale, I think the doctor is trying to be open and honest about what could happen to Scout. Everything has to die, but as he said, it could be years before that happens."

The doctor reassured the boy. "If you see any big changes in Scout's behavior, bring him back in, and we'll check it out."

Dad shook the doctor's hand, while Dale fastened Scout's collar. "Let's get Scout home before you have to meet Mr. Schilke for your lesson and ensemble practice."

Dale sat in the back of the car, quietly petting Scout, who had his head in his lap.

Finally, he was able to verbalize his fears. "I don't like the idea that Scout could die."

Dad sympathized. "I don't blame you. It's never easy losing someone you love. Being raised as a Swede, I learned to look at the death of a loved one a little differently. After a funeral, each of our relatives would tell a story or a fond memory of the deceased. I was taught that a person lives on in the memories of those you leave behind. They may be gone, but we'll keep their memory alive."

"Is that why Grandpa and Grandma are always telling stories about their past?"

"That's right. They want to keep the memories alive for generations to come. If they don't tell them, then they'll be lost forever. Some day, when you have a family of your own, you'll tell them the same stories to honor your ancestors."

"I still don't like thinking about Scout dying. I guess part of growing up is learning how to handle tough situations."

"It's never easy, but it's a part of life that we all have to deal with it at some time. But on a positive note, the doctor did say it could be years before anything happens."

Dale paused and then said, "I guess it's like Mr. Schilke said. You can't control other people or situations ... you can only control your emotions and reactions to them."

They pulled into the driveway to find the gang waiting on the front porch. "Looks like your ensemble is here a little early and can't wait for ... what did you call it?"

"Mr. Schilke called it a master class. Remember, to be early is to be on time and to be on time is to be late," Dale said as he nudged Scout out the back door of the car.

Chapter 24
TENSION BUILDS

It had been four weeks since the conference championship and the quintet's master class with Mr. Schilke. During the practice, they played several new pieces, and he worked them hard to get them to play with more emotion. He stressed preparing for a performance and not letting outside influences affect their playing. Repeatedly, he emphasized treating each rehearsal as though it were a performance.

The quintet had practiced at least once a day for the past four weeks. On the weekends, they would spend extra time practicing. When they believed they were not playing well, they would play from memory so they could focus more on the music and expression. Today, Thursday, February 28, 1946, was the day before the state contest, and emotions were running high.

Mr. Jeffrey delivered his final instructions. "I still need a couple of permission slips. Since the contest is held on a school day, I must have your parents' signed field trip forms before getting on the bus. Each of you must be sure to pack your music, scores for the judges, and folding music stands if you are in an ensemble. Lastly, each number two player or group must be ready at the last minute in case something happens to the number one solo or ensemble. Is that clear?"

"One final item ... Dale, you will remain number two to Jim, although I'm not very happy with his solo preparation. Your quintet, however, will remain number one for the time being. I'll need each event's maximum effort and attention to detail. See you in the morning at 8 a.m. sharp, and enjoy the rest of your day."

As the students began packing up, Dale made sure he had all of his music put away safely in his folder. He checked each of his quintet's folders as well.

P.J. tapped his foot waiting for Dale. "Don't you trust us to pack our own music?"

"Better safe than sorry. You know what's riding on this performance." P.J. sighed, and scooted off to get to his next class.

Dale stopped at the instrument locker room, only to find Jim standing in front of his locker. Dale had no choice but to ask Jim to move aside.

"Can you please move so I can get in my locker? I don't want to be late to class."

Ignoring Dale, Jim took a step back, allowing Dale to open the locker and put his horn away. He double-checked to make sure the lock was secure. As Dale left the band room, Victor joined him.

Dale confided his thoughts about Jim. "It was really strange. He just looked at me and didn't say anything. I'd rather have him say something mean than say nothing at all. His silence gives me the creeps."

Victor consoled his friend. "I think he should worry about his solo, which I don't think sounds so good. He wants to mess with your mind. Remember what Pete told us about the last contest and messing up the finals."

"You might be right, but first we have to get to the finals before we can mess them up."

"Well, tomorrow we'll find out. I hope everyone can relax and just have fun playing," Dale said. "Especially Mr. Jeffrey. He seems really nervous, and when he is nervous that makes us nervous." As the bell rang, the two boys dashed into class.

The rest of the day went quickly, with the gang meeting on the school steps after school.

Chrissy suggested, "How about hanging out at my house and listening to some jazz? I don't want to play my solo or think about my ensemble. I need to clear my head." She pretended to shake her head as if notes were coming out.

Tommy stood, "I agree. If we aren't ready by now, we'll never be."

Bridget grabbed Chrissy and Sandra's hands, and they ran down the steps. The boys followed, all looking forward to a well-deserved break from practicing.

Chapter 25

TRIUMPH OVER ADVERSITY

Early Friday morning, the ride on the school bus to the state music contest in Indianapolis took about an hour. Some students slept, others looked over their music, and a few chatted quietly. The quintet sat together in three seats toward the back. P.J. took one whole seat for himself and slept, drool dripping like a leaky faucet down the side of his mouth, his face pressed against the window. Victor and Karl shared one seat, and across the aisle, Sandra sat with Dale.

"What do you think our chances are today in the first round?" Sandra asked, playing with a lock of her hair.

Dale was uncertain. "I've never been in a contest before. I don't know what to expect."

Sandra nodded. "We've done a really good job getting ready, and I think everyone seems relaxed, especially P.J." She turned and laughed when she saw the drool had dripped onto his shirt. Then Sandra's gray eyes flashed. "You should've had the chance to play your solo. You're definitely playing better than Jim. But for some reason, you seem to let him get to you. What does he do to cause you to react like that?"

Dale leaned back in the seat. "He doesn't have to do much ... a snotty comment here or a look there just gets me riled up. Just the sight of his black eyes and mean face and all the run-ins I've had with him come rushing back."

"I've got an idea. Why don't I be your shadow for the day? When he's around, I'll distract you and keep your mind on our performances, and not what he is thinking or doing."

"You'd do that for me?" He looked at Sandra with a new appreciation. "It's a deal."

"As you boys always say, 'All for one, and one for all.'"

Their laughter woke P.J. from his sleep. Self-consciously, he wiped the slobber off his cheek and rubbed his eyes.

The bus arrived at the contest site. A signboard greeted the arriving bands, wishing them good luck at the competition. The students unloaded their instruments and followed Mr. Jeffrey to their homeroom. It was a classroom in which they could store their horns and music until their performance time. On the way to the room, Mr. Jeffrey pointed out the warm-up room, the auditorium (where they would listen to the final round), the board (where contest results would be posted), and finally the cafeteria (where they could eat and socialize with students from the other schools).

Bridget caught up with Dale and Sandra as they continued down the maze of hallways. "Do you believe all the kids here? I overheard someone say that there were 30 schools and over 900 events in 20 different rooms. This is wild!"

"Once we get to the homeroom, let's find our performance rooms. I think this school is bigger than East."

After finding the homeroom, Mr. Jeffrey gathered the students around him for some final instructions.

"If you need me during the day, I'll either be in the director's lounge or listening to your performances. You should attend as many musical events as possible so you can hear a variety of performances. When you listen to a solo or ensemble, be respectful. They are under enough pressure, so don't add to it. Keep track of your performance times and always warm up and tune carefully. Watch the results, and at the end of the day, report back here to find out if we will have a play-off. You have about thirty minutes now before the contest starts, so find out where you play. Good luck and go lions!"

The students responded with a "ROOAAAAARRRRR" and then poured out of the homeroom to explore the school and find their performance rooms.

At exactly nine o'clock, the contest began. Adrianne was the first event of the day for East Libertyville. Dale wished her well before she went to warm up. "Thanks, Dale. I'd love for you to come listen. You seem to bring me good luck," she said as she fluttered her eyelashes at Dale.

"Are you sure?"

"Absolutely, I can't think of anyone I'd like to perform for more than you. What did you tell me before the last concert? Play to someone you care about, and if you do, that person will know you are playing for them. This time, it's my turn to see if you know who I'm playing for."

Dale blushed as Adrianne dashed to warm up in the warm-up room. Turning around, he came face to face with Jim.

"So Adrianne thinks you're a good luck charm? Well, you're going to need it. Don't mess up your ensemble, or my quintet might have to take your spot in the finals."

Dale stood his ground, but Sandra came to his side. "There you are!" she gushed. "Come on, Mr. Lucky Charm, Adrianne awaits." Giving Jim a sly smile, Sandra whisked Dale out of the room.

In the hallway, Dale took a deep breath. Sandra said, "That's my job today to be your wingman and keep you focused. For whatever reason, I think Adrianne likes you."

"No way; she's an eighth grader who is way too old for me," Dale said, returning to his normal, jovial self.

The flute room was packed, and Adrianne played magnificently. At the end of her solo, she looked at Dale and smiled ever so slightly before approaching the judge. During the rest of the morning, Dale heard other trumpet players from different schools, and even a few brass quintets. But the event Dale and his friends really wanted to hear was their rival ensemble, the West brass quintet that had won last year. As

Dale's quintet made its way through the congested hallway to the West performance room, they accidentally came face to face with the group as they were entering the warm-up room. The three boys from the basketball team saw Dale and shouted, "Hey, Kingston! All for one, and one for all ... but not this time, it's payback time!"

"They sure are friendly," Karl blurted out, causing them to laugh and taking their minds off their upcoming performance.

They settled in the crowded classroom, waiting for the event to start. The West players entered the room with confidence, nodding to other students who had come to watch this premier ensemble. When they finished their performance, the room erupted in applause.

Afterward in the hallway, Dale and his friends had to agree that West's group was very good, but if East performed as they had practiced, they could outscore them. As the day went on, the top two schools were West and East, trading places between first and second.

Dale's group was scheduled to perform, at 2:00. After warming up, they made their way to the contest room. Students from other schools jammed into the room along with the band members from East and West. The members of West's quintet sat in the front row. Dale was the last performer to enter when he felt a soft tap on his shoulder. Adrianne leaned over and whispered, "This time, I'll be your lucky charm." She brushed by him and found a place to stand in the back. Dale stood open-mouthed, until P.J. tugged on his sleeve.

"Let's show these kids what a real brass quintet plays like."

Once the quintet got seated and tuned, they waited for the judge's signal. Scanning the room, Dale noted that Mr. Jeffrey sat in the center. Jim Petris sat next to the director, leaning back in his chair, his arms crossed, as if daring Dale to play well. But what caught Dale's eye was an older man in the back corner who he didn't recognize.

Finally the judge spoke. "This must be East Liberty's Brass Quintet, scheduled to perform at 2:00. Looks like you young people have quite a following. I would like to remind the audience to be quiet until the performance is over." Then the judge told the ensemble that when they were ready, they could begin.

Dale took a deep breath and looked at each player to make sure they were ready. He gave three quick nods of his head, and the group started. As the piece progressed, the audience could feel the emotion and excitement building with each phrase as the piece raced to the end. When the piece climaxed on the last note, the ensemble's eyes were on Dale, waiting for the cut-off. Just as they had practiced, they *crescendoed* until they could get no louder. Dale gave the cut-off with a nod of his head, which was followed by complete silence. Dale looked at the other players, who seem puzzled; but then the silence was broken with shouts of bravo and clapping. Even the judge was clapping, until he caught himself and returned to writing comments on the adjudication sheet.

As they had been taught, the quintet showed no emotion until they were outside the contest room. Then Sandra impulsively threw her arms around Dale and then the other players, giving them hugs. Mr. Jeffrey burst out of the room with a huge smile, congratulating the group for an outstanding performance. Dale spied the older man, who had been sitting in the back jotting notes in a notebook, exit the room and then fade into the crowd of students lugging instruments.

As Jim emerged from the room with his quintet cronies, Sandra swooped in and took Dale by the arm. "That was an amazing performance. Let's go back to the homeroom and put our instruments away."

The contest was slowly coming to an end with only a few events left. Tying their score with West's quintet, Dale's quintet received a Division I and a score of thirty-eight. At this juncture, the two schools were tied.

"What's our last event?" Tommy asked, taking a swig of cola as they sat in the school cafeteria. "If we score higher on this last event, we may not have to have a tie breaker."

"Let me check," Bridget said as she took out her program. "Jim's solo is the last event at 3:15. How about we go hear him?"

Dale admitted, "Well, he did come and hear us, so I guess we owe him the favor."

Sandra interrupted. "Plus, you're a lucky charm," she cooed, imitating Adrianne.

"What's all this lucky charm talk?" P. J. asked innocently as they left the cafeteria in anticipation of the tie-breaking performance.

Word must have spread around the contest that the two schools were tied, and if East's last event earned a Division I, they would win the state contest outright. If not, there would be another round starting at 4:00.

The contest room was standing-room only when Dale and his friends arrived. They squeezed through the rows to stand in the back. Dale watched as Jim entered the room and glanced at Dale. The eyes that were usually so cold and confident somehow seemed different. Studying his face, it dawned on Dale that Jim's eyes reflected raw terror and nerves. Jim looked away quickly and began to tune.

"What's he doing?" Karl whispered. "He's sharp, but he keeps pushing his slide in, making him sharper. Doesn't he remember that if you're sharp you pull out, flat you push in?" Jim got more frustrated with each adjustment to the slide and finally gave up and waited.

The weight of the silence was almost tangible as the audience waited for the judge's signal for the soloist to begin.

Victor leaned into Dale. "If he messes this up, it won't be because of us. I think he's all talk and no action." Dale just held his finger to his lips, quieting Victor. When the judge finished writing his comments from the previous group, he reminded the crowd to be respectful and remain quiet.

"Whenever you are ready, Mr. Petris, you may begin."

Jim took a deep breath, nodded his head to indicate the tempo to his accompanist and began. From the very first note, Jim was in trouble. He had started the piece too fast and was having major intonation problems on his long notes. After the first few minutes, however, he settled down and finished much stronger than he had started.

The crowd politely applauded and began filing out, while Jim stayed to talk with the judge. Mr. Jeffrey told everyone earlier in the day to meet in the homeroom after the last event while they waited for the results. When Dale and his friends entered the homeroom, the band members joined the nervous chatter as they waited to hear if they had won. The students who had not heard Jim's solo were anxious to hear the results, but the general consensus was that it didn't go well. After about ten minutes, Jim slunk in with Adrianne consoling him.

Sandra was not sympathetic. "I don't feel sorry for him at all. All he's done is talk about how good he is and intimidates us, especially you. I know that may be mean, but if he's going to talk tough, then he better back it up with a great performance."

"I don't trust Adrianne either," Chrissy added, looking directly at Dale. "She acts all nice, but will do anything or say anything to get ahead."

"Enough mean talk. Let's just hope the judge gave him the benefit of the doubt and awarded him a Division I so we can win." Before anyone could answer, a loud cheer erupted from the homeroom next door—West Libertyville's.

Mr. Jeffrey walked briskly into the room, closing the door behind him. "You probably guessed by the cheering next door that our last solo did not earn a Division I, so now we're tied. I need to select the group to play the tie breaker in the auditorium. I've already heard that West will send the quintet that beat us last year. I'm not going to make that mistake again. Since Dale's quintet matched West's score today, they are the ones to bring home the state trophy. If the eighth graders are disappointed about not being picked, I understand, but I want you to support them in the best interests of our school."

Dale looked over at Jim who was fuming for getting a two on his solo, thus not getting to play the finals and redeem himself. Jim motioned to Dale and ran his finger across his throat.

Mr. Jeffrey jolted Dale back into reality. "I want the seventh-grade brass quintet to get some water and relax in the cafeteria for a few minutes before we move into the auditorium. Then you'll return to warm up before the finals at 4:00. The contest manager will send a runner before you play. Good luck!"

Gathered together in the cafeteria, the quintet talked about how they might improve on their previous performance. The fifteen minutes went quickly, and they returned to warm up. As they entered the homeroom, the room was eerily quiet. The students had taken their horns and folders with them to the auditorium, leaving only the group's horns and music. Dale sensed something was amiss, but he couldn't put his finger on it until he got his horn out and began warming up.

"Let's run a little bit of the song to calm my nerves," Sandra said, taking out her music.

Dale moved around the room, looking under each desk and chair.

"What are you looking for?" Sandra said.

"My folder is missing. It was right under my case when we left. You don't think someone picked it up by mistake?"

"Relax ... it's here," P.J. said, laying his tuba down. The others searched the room to no avail when the contest runner knocked on the door and announced, "Ten minutes until we walk to the auditorium. Make your final preparations."

Dale sank down into a chair. "It was here." He was at a loss of what to do, until Sandra had an idea.

"We can turn this in our favor. The piece we played earlier only tied with West. Why don't we stand and play a different piece from memory? I have the judge's score in my folder. Dale, you can look at the score as a quick review."

"But Mr. Jeffrey wants us to play the same piece. He will be furious," Karl pleaded.

Dale realized Sandra was right. "We don't have a choice. This isn't about Mr. Jeffrey. It's about us turning a negative into a positive. I don't have any music, we need to find an edge against West, and we've played this piece before from memory. As I recall, we played even better without music."

Victor raised his arm in the center of the room. "Dale, you know the answer." And, they all shouted, "All for one, and one for all!"

Next door, the West ensemble with the three boys from the basketball team heard the muffled phrase they remembered well. "I don't like the sound of that," Bill murmured before resuming their warm-up.

Sandra got out her part and the score to the piece they would play from memory and went over it quickly with Dale. Each player worked with Dale, pointing out parts in the score that helped trigger Dale's memory.

"I'm ready. Let's tune and take the stage like lions!" P.J. growled, "Roooooooooooaaaaaaaaaaar to success."

In the next room, the West ensemble heard the commotion. "What do you think is going on? They're acting like it's a sport event. If they think they can intimidate us, they have another thing coming."

The runners knocked on both doors simultaneously, announcing it was time for the final round.

Dale advised the group before they exited the room. "Remember what Mr. Schilke told us—worry about what you can control, stand tall, look the part, show no fear, and play expressively." He looked earnestly at each of his friends. "When I play my part, I'm playing for each one of you, the best friends ever."

As the two groups moved from the homeroom to the auditorium on opposite sides of the hallway, the West group took notice.

"Hey, Kingston! You forgot your music," one of them said as he laughed and walked down the hall.

Dale gestured at his head, "No, I didn't ... it's right here."

Startled, the first West player came to a stop, and the others bumped into him. Then they continued to the backstage of the auditorium.

The runner took the scores for the judges from each group. The other runner reminded the two groups that when they went onstage, they should tune first, and then wait for the judge to announce their school and the title of the piece they would perform.

"According to the rules, last year's winners have a choice to perform first or second. West, what's your choice?"

The group looked at one another, and then Bill stepped forward. "We'll play first, so East can hear what a state-winning group sounds like."

"OK, East will go second." The runner showed them where to wait backstage until it was time for their performance.

Sandra spoke for the ensemble. "When West is done, just clear the stage of all chairs and stands. We won't need them."

The runner looked confused. "I'm not sure that is allowed in the rules. I'll have to check."

The runner talked with a tall older man standing backstage. Dale recognized him as the man who was in the back of their room during their earlier performance.

The runner returned. "It's allowed in the rules ... and I have to say, this is one performance I can't wait to hear."

The West players moved out into the bright lights onstage to generous applause.

Dale huddled his group together in a corner of the backstage area. "I want to focus on our performance, not theirs. Don't forget to make a shallow half-circle so we can see each other. P. J. is the middle with Sandra on the left end, and I'll be on the right. Karl is next to Sandra and Victor is next to me."

Dale was interrupted by thunderous applause, signaling that West had completed their performance.

"East, you're next. Give us just a minute to clear the stage."

Dale looked each player in the eye. "Remember, no matter what happens, we've earned the right to play, so let's enjoy it. Make a memory today that will last a lifetime!"

The ensemble formed a line behind the edge of the stage curtain. They watched the audience as they waited for the stage to be cleared. Students, directors, and parents were pointing and talking animatedly. In the center row, they could see their fellow East band mates and Mr. Jeffrey, who raised his hands in frustration as the stage was cleared entirely. Dale could see Jim sitting in the front, holding something black against his chest. Squinting in the bright stage lights, Dale saw something that made his blood boil. It was a folder with the number 46: his folder number. *Control the things you can*, he repeated to himself.

"East, you may take the stage."

The group took the stage confidently as if they owned it. They made a slight curved half circle and tuned. Once satisfied, they calmly faced the audience, waiting for a sign from the judges to continue.

"Are the judges ready?" the announcer asked. One by one, the three judges signaled they were ready.

Dale looked one last time at the group, checking to make sure they were ready, and stepped forward and said, "We are the brass quintet from East Libertyville Junior High, and we will be playing the *Sonata* from *Die Bankelsangerlieder*." Before turning back to the ensemble, Dale held out his hand and pointed at Jim in the audience, signaling *I know what you did, and you aren't going to win*. The crowd politely applauded. Dale could see Mr. Jeffrey looking intently at the players onstage, his lips pursed into a tight line.

Dale took a deep breath and raised his cornet to his lips. He made eye contact with the other players and gave the three head nods to start … and start they did. Dale's opening phrase was strong and confident and set the tone for the remainder of the song. Each player relaxed and played their hearts out for one another. As the song built to the final phrase, Dale sensed that the group wanted to start softer and *crescendo* more than usual.

It all started when P.J. played his driving bass line forcefully and softly. The other players responded, mimicking his dynamics and building in intensity. When Dale hit his last entrance, their eyes met, encouraging the players to let it all out for the final bars. The level of emotion soared, supported by each instrument to the last note, filling the auditorium with the most glorious sound.

Once Dale gave the cut-off, the players held their horns up for a brief moment and looked at one another, realizing they had done something special. When they brought their horns down, the audience burst into applause and shouts of bravo were followed by a standing ovation. Even the West ensemble rose to their feet, acknowledging a great performance.

Offstage, tears filled Sandra's eyes as she hugged each player, Dale being last. She whispered in his ear, "Thanks for stepping up. You took control today."

Dale hugged her back. "Thanks for believing in me."

They agreed that they didn't care what the results were. The experience of a great performance was all that mattered.

Wanting to make sure that the other members of the ensemble recognized his contribution, P.J. puffed out his chest and said, "What did you think about me adding the dynamics at the end?"

Their excitement was interrupted when they heard the announcer ask for quiet.

"The judges have finished tabulating the scores. This has been one of the most exciting finals we've ever had. Both groups should be commended on two outstanding performances." The auditorium exploded with their applause of approval.

"Will the two ensembles please join me onstage." Both groups walked onstage, with one group on each side of the announcer. "First, let me congratulate you both on two great performances ... and now the scores. The first group to perform, West Libertyville Junior High, earned a score of 38.5." The crowd remained silent, waiting to hear the second number.

"The score for East Libertyville is"... and the announcer paused, as if taunting the audience, "39.9." East, you are the new state champions! Congratulations!"

The applause was deafening. Dale and the ensemble had decided not to celebrate onstage if they had won and to shake the hands of the West players, congratulating them on a great final. When Dale got to the three basketball players, they all came up at the same time and shook Victor's and his hands. "We thought you would be a couple of self-centered kids, but we think you're team players both on and off the floor. With our two schools' talent coming together in high school, we'll have more state music and basketball championships in our future."

After the congratulations onstage, the group walked quietly back to the homeroom to pack up and meet the band at the buses. Mr. Jeffrey met them as they entered the room. "First, congratulations on an amazing performance, but you have some explaining to do about your selection of music."

Karl, who was usually soft-spoken, squarely faced his director. "I think you should ask Jim about our choice of music. Right now, we're going to celebrate and let the explanations wait until Monday."

Mr. Jeffrey was stunned, but replied. "OK ... meet the band at the buses."

After Mr. Jeffrey left, Sandra was on Karl. "What got into you?"

"When I saw Dale point at Jim and could see the folder number, I thought, there's no way I'm going to let that kid continue to hassle not only Dale, but also us. I sort of lost it."

P.J. agreed. "Leave the explanations until Monday. It's time to celebrate on the bus." He swung his tuba over his shoulder and headed for the buses. "I hope this will earn me some hugs from the girls."

Sandra and Dale were the last ones out. "Sandra, I want to tell you ..."

"Don't say anything. That's what friends are for." Grabbing Dale's hand and dragging him down the hall, they ran to the buses to celebrate the school's first-ever state music championship.

Chapter 26

FINAL SACRIFCE

Dale rolled over to look at his alarm clock. Could it really be ten o'clock in the morning? The celebration on the bus and then in the band room had been memorable, with P.J. getting lots of hugs. The band was finally able to relax after eight weeks of hard work. Numerous band students asked the quintet about playing from memory, but they brushed those off, not wanting to ruin the victory.

When the band room cleared, Chrissy invited the gang to her house for some colas and snacks. She had called her parents, who contacted the other parents to get permission for the party that went late into the night. They played jazz, danced, and talked about the exciting day, sharing the reason for having to play from memory. Tommy, Bridget, Bobby, Dave, and Chrissy were furious at Jim for risking the group's chances at a state contest.

"This is the last straw," Tommy vowed. "If you don't tell Mr. Jeffrey, then I will."

"I hear you, but I'm not sure how to approach Mr. Jeffrey."

Bridget intervened. "I think Mr. Jeffrey already started to approach it. I saw Mr. Jeffrey and Jim in the office when we got back, and the conversation looked rather heated. I don't know what happened, but when Jim came out, he gave you a dirty look and left before the celebration was over. I don't like it."

Dale didn't want to discuss the incident further. "I'm exhausted. Do you realize it's two o'clock in the morning?" Shortly, parents began arriving, and the friends said their good-byes. Dale only had to walk across the street and was the last to leave.

Chrissy walked Dale to the porch. The evening was unseasonably warm for this time of year. She slid her hand in his and looked up into his brown eyes.

"I want you to know that I believe in you. It's time to confront this issue head on. Think about it this weekend, and then let's talk after church." She gave him a hug and stepped back. "Don't answer me now ... just think about it. See you on Sunday," she said and she went inside.

The next morning, Dale lay in his bed, patting Scout, who snuggled next to him. "How about you lay in the sun on the back porch while I go for a run and clear my head? I've got a lot to think about." Scout hopped slowly off the bed and headed down the back stairs with Dale following in his workout clothes.

Dale left Scout on the porch as he ran down the steps. He yelled back, "See ya soon!" He felt comforted by the familiar bark as he disappeared down the alley behind his house. He headed to Simpson Hill for the first of three trips up and down. Dale was feeling better by the end of the third trip and was returning home, when Jim stepped out of the weeds that lined the alley, a mean-looking bulldog growling and pulling on a leash by his side. Dale stopped about twenty feet away, angry with himself for not paying more attention to his surroundings. Jim moved toward Dale, the dog baring its teeth and straining the leash.

Dale backed up and shouted. "Call off your dog. I haven't done anything to you."

Jim snarled, "The only thing you've done is make a fool out of me in front of my friends. You've turned them against me. Even Mr. Jeffrey is upset with me. Did you tell him I was pushing you around, you little weasel?" Jim approached Dale, allowing his dog to lunge forward.

Dale moved back a few more steps. "You're the one making yourself look bad. You hassle me and my friends, intimidate the girls, and you made a fool of yourself by performing badly. So you're blaming me for this?"

Jim didn't answer. Instead, he leaned down and put his hand on the dog's collar. "Do you remember the time your dog chased me and my friends up a tree? Well, I want you to keep your mouth shut come Monday. To my point, let's see how fast you are." Jim unclipped the leash.

Dale froze as the bulldog charged full force, the dog's powerful legs digging into the gravel of the alley. At that moment, out of the tall grass, a flash of black and white sprang into the air, colliding with the bulldog just as it leapt to attack Dale.

"Scooouuuut!" Dale yelled as he stumbled backwards. The two dogs fell to the ground, wrestling and snapping, their ears laid back and eyes bulging. Tufts of fur flew as they clawed one another.

Scout flipped the bulldog on its back and sunk his teeth into its neck, pinning the dog to the ground. The bulldog writhed on the gravel, trying to break free. Each time the bulldog tried to escape, Scout would growl, shaking his head and sinking his teeth deeper into the dog's flesh.

Both boys watched the fight in horror. Finally, the bulldog whimpered submissively as he lay limply on the ground, Scout's front paws holding him firmly.

Jim started to approach, but Scout flashed his teeth, emitting a low growl, refusing to release the dog. Dale could hear shouts and the pounding of feet on the gravel. Jim turned and ran back into the weeds, abandoning the scene as Dale's dad ran up.

Dad approached the dogs cautiously. "Dale, don't get near that dog … let me handle it," he said, picking up a hefty stick. "When I pin the dog's neck down, you pull Scout off. I don't think the dog is going to want another fight, but we'll go slowly."

Dad jabbed the stick under the dog's collar. Then Dale pulled Scout off, leaving the bulldog panting and bloody. Once Scout was off to the side, Dale turned his attention to the other dog. Dad released the pressure on the stick. For a few seconds the dog didn't move, but then realizing he was free, he flipped back up and slinked off into the weeds where his master had disappeared.

"Are you all right, Dale? I heard all this shouting and dogs barking, and I knew something was wrong."

Dale was still breathing heavily, leaning forward as if he were going to throw up. "I'm OK ... " he gasped, "but if it hadn't been for Scout, I'd ... " He stopped in mid-sentence as he looked back toward Scout.

The dog, which had just a moment ago saved his life, now lay motionless on the gravel. Dale ran over to his pet and dropped to his knees. Desperately, he pulled Scout's lifeless body onto his lap, burying his face in the dog's damp fur, waiting for Scout to lick his face or bark. There was no response. Dale lifted his tear-stained face toward his father, but there was nothing he could do.

Chapter 27
SAYING GOOD-BYE

There was no need to call the vet. Scout had died protecting his master with the last bit of life he had. Dale laid Scout in his wagon and pulled him into the garage. He gently covered him with his favorite blanket and sat beside his trusted friend in the solitude of the garage. His family sat quietly on the porch discussing what had happened.

"We should call the police and report this. This has gone on long enough and needs to stop," Grandmother said emphatically.

Dad shook his head. "We haven't heard the full story yet, so let's not rush into anything. Let's focus on Dale, and for that matter, all of us having to deal with Scout dying," he said, wiping his eyes. "We all loved that dang dog." He looked up to see Chrissy coming across the driveway.

Mother stood. "Stay here. Let me be the one to tell her."

Chrissy knew something was wrong. "Has something happened to Dale?" she asked anxiously.

Mother shook her head. "Dale's fine, but Scout died protecting him." Putting her arms around Chrissy, she said softly, "You'll have to be brave when you talk to Dale. He needs his friends right now. I know how much you mean to each other and that you loved Scout as much as he did."

Chrissy wept as Mrs. Kingston held her tight. After a few minutes, Chrissy composed herself. "Can I talk to him?"

Mother motioned toward the garage. "He's in there with Scout. I'm sure he would appreciate seeing you."

Chrissy slowly approached the open garage. Dale sat grief-stricken next to the wagon. He looked up, but said nothing. Chrissy realized that words would be pointless, so she sat down next to him and encircled her arms around her best friend. They sat in silence for several minutes before Dale could speak.

"Could you call the gang? I can't. On Sunday, I'm going to bury Scout at the fort. If they want to say good-bye then, they can."

Chrissy promised. "We'll meet you on the porch at ten o'clock. We'll have our own church service for Scout."

She squeezed Dale's hand and ran back home to call the gang and tell them the horrible news.

Dale decided to come out of the garage. His mother, father, and grandparents were still on the porch. They watched solemnly as Dale tentatively approached. "Before dealing with what happened today, I want you to let me bury Scout. I know you're concerned, but I'm asking you to do it my way."

He outlined his plan. First, he wanted to skip church tomorrow so he and his friends could bury Scout at the fort. Then he wanted to spend the night at the fort with Scout for the last time. Mother protested about sleeping alone at the fort, but Dad intervened.

"If Dale wants to spend the night at the fort as a way of dealing with this situation, that's fine with me. He can skip school on Monday, giving us time to discuss what to do. Sometimes a young man has to be alone with his thoughts. I remember after losing good soldiers and friends in battle wanting to be alone with my thoughts."

Grandpa stood. "I have been there myself and agree. Dale, do you remember the bugle I showed you the first time we opened the trunk?"

"Wasn't it the one you played at Teddy Roosevelt's funeral? The one you said should never be played again?"

"That's the one. I think it's time to be played again ... this time for Scout. He earned that right having served his country in the military's *Dogs for Defense* program. I also have a flag from that funeral. Teddy Roosevelt was a special friend and so was Scout. It would serve me proud if you would cover Scout in it when you take him to the fort."

Grandma wiped her eyes.

"You know, C.H., you're a special man. In fact, all my men are special. Come here and give me a hug. I'm going to miss that crazy dog," she said hugging Dale, then C.H., and finally Jake.

Chapter 28

MEMORIES

Sunday dawned bright and sunny with clear blue skies. Dale sat on the porch sipping coffee with his father, waiting for his friends to arrive.

"Thanks for letting me spend the night with Scout. I know Mom doesn't like it, but it'll help."

"Did you pack everything you need?"

"I think so. I've got food, a sleeping bag, matches, water, and a watch."

Dale stood and swung the bugle his grandfather had given him over his shoulder in the leather carrying case. His friends, including P.J.'s dog Smokey, were waiting at the curb. After a brief discussion, Dale ran to the garage and got on his bike, pulling the flag-draped wagon with Scout behind him. The procession continued down the street, with Dale's friends falling in behind on their bicycles. Dale glanced over his shoulder to see his father and grandfather standing at attention on the porch, saluting as they rode away.

Word spread about Scout's death. People on their way to church stopped as the wagon and line of bikes passed by. Some saluted. Others bowed their heads out of respect to the dog that had given his life for his master.

Once they reached the jungle, they had to abandon their bikes and carry Scout to the fort over the rough path that Scout had run on for years. When they arrived at the fort, Dale found that his friends had already dug a grave up on the hill by Scout's favorite tree that he always laid under when the weather was hot. A fire had been laid for the night and the fort was swept clean for his stay.

Dale looked at his friends in gratitude. "Here's what I want to do. We'll bury Scout and then spend the afternoon doing all the things we always do together. At sunset, I'll play *Taps*, and then we can build a fire and sit around telling stories about Scout. My grandfather says telling stories preserves the life of the one who has died. Scout is gone, but I want his memory to live forever."

Victor, P.J., Tommy, Dave, and Karl gently carried Scout's body to the grave. Chrissy, Bridget, and Sandra readied the headstone, which was made from a big white, flat rock they had decorated with Scout's name and dog tag number, C4602. Chrissy had painted a small American flag in the center. Then they covered the grave with dirt.

Dale stood at the foot of the grave. "Let's pray." They lowered their heads. After a few minutes, Dale looked up. "Amen." Then he bravely forced a smile for the first time since Scout's death and said, "Scout loved this place and loved to play, so let's keep that memory alive."

The gang spent the rest of the afternoon playing by the fort, trying to keep their minds off of Scout. The sun set as they returned to the fort. Dale got the bugle out and played *Taps* as the sun slowly slipped behind the surrounding hills. When he finished, the boys started a fire and readied the food they had brought. Smokey came over to Dale and laid his head in his lap.

As they sat around the campfire, the friends reminisced about Scout. Chrissy told of giving Scout belly rubs, and P.J. remembered how Smokey and Scout would play at the fire station. Victor remembered Scout running messages back and forth during games of Capture the Flag. The stories were nonstop and helped them realize that although Scout was gone, his memory would remain with them forever.

"Dale, we'd better get home before our parents get worried," Victor said. The girls hugged Dale, and the boys shook his hand.

"Where is Smokey?" P.J. searched inside the fort.

"Look, over at the grave," Dale said. There was Smokey, his head on his paws, lying atop the mound of dirt under the tree.

"P.J., can Smokey spend the night with me?"

His friend agreed and said wisely, "You both need each other tonight."

After a few more tearful hugs from the girls, the group disappeared down the trail, leaving Dale alone with Smokey. Dale tossed some wood on the fire, sat down next to Scout's grave, and patted Smokey. "It's time for me to work this out."

The night sky was particularly dark, with no stars or a shining moon above. In the distance, Dale could see flashes of lightning and hear rumbles of thunder.

"Sounds like we're going to have a storm tonight," Dale said, checking his watch in the light from the fire. "Midnight. Come on, Smokey, let's go inside." Taking the dog by the collar, he led him to the wooden structure, where they would spend the night.

A flash of lightning illuminated the fort. He gazed out the door at the grave, the white headstone standing out against the dark earth. "I love you, Scout."

Chapter 29

FORK IN THE ROAD

Dale lay awake in his sleeping bag with Smokey curled up next to him, listening to the approaching storm. With each flash and accompanying thunder, Dale thought about how he'd grown up in some ways and didn't take responsibility for solving problems in other ways.

The sky flashed. "One, one thousand one," Dale recited until he reached twenty-five before the thunder rumbled. His grandfather had taught him how to estimate the distance of a storm. *Five seconds per mile, so this storm is five miles away.*

Another flash interrupted his thoughts; "One, one-thousand one … " He counted to twenty before the thunder arrived. In his mind, Dale saw himself kneeling to hug Scout in farewell at the train station, tearfully sending him to become a messenger dog in the *Dogs for Defense* program. *Four miles away.*

Another strike flashed, this one brighter than the one before. "One, one-thousand one ... " Dale counted to fifteen before the thunder jolted the fort. He visualized meeting Jim on the steps of the junior high for the first time. A crack of thunder popped, even closer now. *Only three miles now.*

Through the fort's window, Dale saw the zigzag of lightning. "One, one-thousand one ... " He only counted to ten before the thunder boomed. *Only two miles.* He thought of how Jim and his friends confronted him in the park and how Scout protected him, chasing them up the tree and tearing Jim's pocket off.

Another bolt of lightning streaked across the sky. "One, one-thousand one ... " Now he got to five before the next crack of thunder arrived, shaking the ground and the fort. Dale thought about Jim sabotaging his horn and messing up his audition for chairs, and how he had not said anything. *Only one mile*, Dale thought as his heart began to pound, his anger was becoming increasingly intense with each additional flash.

Flash! "One ... " Crack! The storm had arrived. The rain relentlessly pelted the thin walls of the fort. The flashes and memories were coming so fast that he closed his eyes and pulled the sleeping bag over his head, hoping to fend off the memories.

Finally, he could take it no more. He jerked to an upright position, looked up at the storm, and screamed, "Scooouuuuut!" as the torment of Scout's last heroic action, the blurred black and white fur flying through the air to protect his master, exploded in his head. Dale climbed out of the sleeping bag and opened the door to the fort. His shirt was soaked in sweat and his breathing heavy. He braced his hands against the doorframe, reliving the final moments of Scout's life.

A bolt of lightning flashed directly above the tree by Scout's grave. Momentarily, Dale was blinded, seeing a halo of white light surrounding the tree. The clap of thunder left his ears ringing.

Dale staggered backwards a few steps, but then he found his balance. He straightened his shoulders and stood tall against the driving rain that strafed his body. With a new resolve, he looked up at the fast-moving clouds. "I predict there'll be another storm in the morning."

Just as quickly as the storm had arrived, it moved down the valley and away from the fort. The first light of morning peaked under the departing clouds. As the sky cleared, so did Dale's mind. He knew exactly what he had to do.

"Come on, Smokey. Let's see the damage." He opened the door, and what he saw confirmed the power of the storm. The lightning split Scout's favorite tree down the middle, the two halves forming the letter Y. Dale paused. *This is a sign. This is the fork in the road.* He had a choice of which fork to take: either face his issues, or continue to be manipulated and bullied for the rest of his life.

Dale leaned down and gave Smokey a hug. Smokey licked Dale's face in return and barked twice as if saying. "It's OK ... but it's time to step up."

Chapter 30

STEPPING UP

Dale pedaled furiously toward the firehouse with Smokey bounding by his side. He was soaked from the rain, his clothes and face smeared with mud, and he smelled of smoke from the campfire. He chained Smokey outside the firehouse.

Dale glanced at his watch. It was 7:45—time to get moving. He took the back alleys to the junior high. He knew that most of the students would be inside by the time he got to the school. He waited in the alley across the street from East, out of sight, until he heard the bell ring. He hurried across the street, parked his bike, and ran in the side door next to the band hall. The hall was empty, all the students in class. Dale's wet shoes squished as he walked down the hall toward the band room. He could hear the band warming up on the chorale he loved *Wach auf, mein Herz*, which meant *Wake Up, My Heart*.

Dale hesitated as he listened to the song. "Stay calm, finish this." He opened the door and walked in undetected. He stood in the front of the room, wet and muddy, his chest heaving.

Adrianne saw Dale first and screamed, putting her hand over her mouth. The band stopped playing abruptly as Mr. Jeffrey turned to see what had caused the disruption.

"Dale, is that you? What happened? Are you OK?" Mr. Jeffrey rapidly fired questions as he jumped off the podium and approached the boy.

"Mr. Jeffrey … please stay on the podium. I have something to say," Dale said tensely, holding up his hand.

Mr. Jeffrey hesitated before inching toward Dale. "This isn't like you. I need to call the office."

Dale moved toward Mr. Jeffrey with his hand still up. "Please, do not get off the podium. I want you and the rest of the band to hear this. You owe me that much. Just stand and listen."

Dale didn't wait for a reply. He reached inside his shirt and pulled Scout's dog tags off his neck. He gripped them tightly in his fist and held them up for all to see.

"I've let Jim bully me for the last year, and I've never told you, Mr. Jeffrey. In fact, he has systematically intimidated my friends, his own quintet, and numerous other members of this band."

Jim shouted out, "That's a lie. You're the one who bullied me."

Mr. Jeffrey intervened. "This is not the time for this, Dale."

"Yes, it is ... and you're part of the problem." Mr. Jeffrey started to say something. "Let me finish. When I first came here to audition, Jim threatened my friends and me. Then he disrupted my final sight-reading. Do you remember?"

"Yes ... but."

Dale cut off the director. "Then he and his friends tried to intimidate me in the alley behind my house. They smashed my Victory Garden and threatened me again in the park during the end of the war celebration. Ring a bell, Jim?" Jim vigorously shook his head in denial.

"That's only the beginning. How about the time you tricked me into getting the folder that first rehearsal? Then you stuck an eraser in my lead pipe before my audition. Do you remember that, Mr. Jeffrey?"

"That's a lie," Jim shouted.

Holding up the dog tags with the eraser still attached, Dale continued. "Take the pencil out of your folder, the one that doesn't have an eraser."

Mr. Jeffrey looked down at the podium. "Dale, I didn't know."

"How could you, Mr. Jeffrey, when you're constantly pressuring us to compete for chairs, section leaders, being number one for solos, and driving us to win some trophy that has nothing to do with the love of playing our horns? You created such tension that you lost the ability to see what was going on. If you don't believe me, ask Pete, Mike, Joe, Adrianne, or any other band member. They'll tell you I'm right.

But, here is the part you don't know about Jim. You asked us why we played without music to win the state contest. Do you want to tell him, Jim? Do you want to be a man and fess up, or do I have to tell him?"

"What are you taking about?" Jim feigned innocence.

"I'll tell you," Dale said, taking a step closer to Jim. "Jim stole my folder right before the final round. Then he had the nerve to sit in the front row so we'd see it when we came onstage."

"Is that true?" Mr. Jeffrey studied Jim's face.

"I'm not done. You remember the next part, don't you, Jim? The part where I'm out running, letting off steam the day after contest, and you sic your dog on me." Squeezing Scout's dog tags for support, Dale continued. "You said I'd made a fool out of you in front of your friends and turned them against you. Oh, and what was your final threat before you released your dog? Something like, I'd better keep my mouth shut and not tattle to Mr. Jeffrey about you pushing me around?"

The band room was completely silent. Mr. Jeffrey stared at Dale, his mouth forming a tight line.

"What's caused me to finally confront you was Scout dying to save me from your dog. When you heard my dad coming, you ran home and didn't see us release your dog and Scout dying in my lap."

Dale squared his shoulders, his eyes blazing at Jim. "If my dog can stand up to you, then why shouldn't I?" Turning back to Mr. Jeffrey, Dale unleashed his fury. "All of this bullying has been because Jim thinks he's a better player than me. I want you to select any part … etude, scales … you name it. I want to put this bullying to an end without any fighting. I want to challenge Jim in front of the band—winner takes all. If he plays better than me, he can keep the first chair. But if I win, he has to leave me and everyone else alone and take responsibility for his actions."

"Dale, this isn't the time or place for this."

"I don't care what you think. I do care about what the band thinks, and what I think. Let them decide."

Pete stood up. "Sorry, Mr. Jeffrey, Dale is right. Let them play." Other players followed suit, standing and shouting out to let them play. Finally, it was so loud, Mr. Jeffrey held up his hand for quiet.

"OK, if the band agrees, then fine. Dale, go get your horn. Adrianne, get a stand for Dale and his folder."

"Not Adrianne," Dale said quickly. "Chrissy!" By the time Dale returned with his horn, Chrissy had the stand and music set up in the front of the room.

"Do you want to warm up?"

"No. Let's do this."

Mr. Jeffrey explained the process. "We'll do two different sight-reading selections. I'll give each of you one minute to look the piece over, and then you'll play it straight through. Jim will go first on the first selection, and Dale, you will go first on the second selection. When both are done, the band will decide the winner."

Each player took turns practicing and playing the sight-reading. When Dale finished his last note, he looked into Jim's eyes and smiled.

Mr. Jeffrey said to the band. "Let's vote. Raise your hand if you think Jim won." Adrianne quickly raised her hand. She looked around to see that she was the only one with her hand raised. "OK, raise your ..." but Mr. Jeffrey never got to finish before all hands except Adrianne's shot in the air.

"This isn't fair! I was set up, and Dale's the bully, not me," Jim shouted over the cheers of the band students.

"Jim, I'd like to see you in my office immediately. Dale, you wait outside until I call you in. I want to get to the bottom of this. Class dismissed."

Chrissy took Dale's cornet from him and put it in his locker. Dale turned his back to the risers to thank Chrissy. Out of the corner of her eye, she saw Jim running toward Dale. She screamed.

Dale heard the pounding feet and knew what was coming. He turned to find Jim two feet away, his fist clinched and arm pulled back. Remembering what his father had taught him, Dale reacted without thinking. As the punch came, he grabbed Jim's fist, pushing it up and away from him, exposing Jim's chest. Dale drove his shoulder into his attacker's chest, using his balance and Jim's forward motion to flip Jim over his head, sending him crashing to the floor on his back. Still holding Jim's fist, he twisted it back and pinned him down securely to the floor. Dale remembered, *Hold until help arrives,* and applied more pressure to make sure Jim couldn't get up.

In seconds, Mr. Jeffrey was on the scene and separated the two. Principal Hamilton, who was in the hallway and heard the scream, burst through the door to help.

"Mr. Jeffrey, you take Jim, and I'll take Dale," he said brusquely. They escorted the two boys out of the band room in front of the stunned band students.

Chapter 31
CONSEQUENCES

Dale sat in the waiting room of Mr. Hamilton's office wiping the mud from his face with a towel they had given him. His dad was sitting quietly next to him. He could hear the muffled voices of Mr. Hamilton, Mr. Jeffrey, Jim, and Jim's mom through the walls, but he couldn't make out what they were saying. Dale looked up to see Jim and his mom leave the office through the side door and walk down the hall.

"You do know they'll punish both of you, don't you?" asked Dale's father.

Dale nodded solemnly. "I'm sorry, Dad. I knew that, but I never thought it would end with Jim attacking me. I didn't throw the first punch. I just defended myself."

The principal's door opened. "Dale and Mr. Kingston, you can come in now."

Dale had never been in the principal's office before, and he knew that you didn't get in there unless you were in trouble.

"Have a seat, and let's get to the bottom of this. Mr. Jeffrey explained what you did this morning and that he witnessed Jim attack you. He said you defended yourself. Do you have anything else to say?"

Dale was sorrowful, his voice quavering. "First, I'm sorry for causing all this trouble today, Mr. Jeffrey. I didn't want it to end like this. I thought a lot during the last two days about how to handle my problem. I could've done it a dozen different ways, but I just finally had to step up and face Jim myself, right or wrong."

"Why didn't you tell someone about this before it got out of hand?"

Dad cleared his throat. "Let me answer that, Dale. It all began while I was away in the Pacific. Dale didn't want to worry his mother or grandparents. When I got back in September, Dale told me most everything, and eventually we told his mom and grandparents. We tried to teach him different ways to deal with bullies. He wanted to handle it himself and not be seen as a tattletale. Sure, we could have told you and Mr. Jeffrey, but after seeing how Jim reacted, I'm not sure that would have helped."

Mr. Jeffrey interrupted. "Dale, do you really think I contributed to this? You said so in front of the band."

Dale glanced at his dad who nodded for him to answer.

"Yes, but I don't think you did it on purpose. I felt pressure and so did the other band students. You didn't see the signs, and I was afraid ... or confused ... about how to tell you about Jim."

"Let's try and keep the focus on Dale and not on Mr. Jeffrey," Mr. Hamilton said. "We have a no fighting policy, which I'm sure you're aware of. No matter who starts a fight, both students receive the same punishment. I have no choice but to suspend you from school for five days beginning immediately. You may return next Monday, and before you're allowed back in class, you'll meet with me, Jim, your counselor Miss Culver, and Mr. Jeffrey. Is that clear?"

"Yes, I understand ... but what about the concert in three weeks and the trumpet trio we're getting ready for?"

"You should have thought about that earlier, but don't worry about that right now," Mr. Jeffrey said. "We'll work that out later."

Mr. Hamilton directed Dale to take his books home, empty his band locker, and go home with his father before the next passing period. "I'll see you next Monday at 7:30 a.m. in this office. Is that clear?"

Dale and his dad rode home in silence. They pulled into the driveway and sat in the car. Finally, Dale spoke. "Did I do wrong today? Do you think I could have done it differently?"

"Now that this situation has played out, I think we all could have handled it another way."

"Who is all?"

"Well, for starters ... you. You could have come forward and told Mr. Jeffrey and Mr. Hamilton, but then who knows how that would've worked out. Mr. Jeffrey could have seen the obvious signs and been more proactive. Finally, I could've spoken to both Mr. Jeffrey and Mr. Hamilton with you, rather than letting you deal with this on your own. I think Jim has some major anger issues that need to be resolved. This isn't about who plays better. There's more to it than that." Dad opened the car door. "We'll discuss it further when we sit down for dinner."

"When Mom comes home from work, do you think I'll be in trouble?"

"I think both of us are already in trouble," he said, looking over at the porch, Grandma and Grandpa sitting stiffly on the porch swing. "Go on, face the music, and then go get cleaned up."

Chapter 32

TRUTH COMES OUT

Sitting at the dinner table, Dale explained what had caused the confrontation with Jim in the band room to his mother and grandparents, who sat quietly listening.

"When I was at the fort thinking about Scout and the last year, I realized I had let myself and others down by not standing up to Jim and having more self-respect. During the storm, I decided to put an end to this game, which wasn't about Jim as much as it was about me not standing up for myself. I realized that night I had a choice to grow up and believe in myself and my friends, or to lead a life of being intimidated and bullied."

Dale's mom leaned forward, resting her elbows on the table. "Do you think you could have handled this in a different way?"

"Sure … but at the time, it seemed the best way. I've grown up in so many ways during the last year. I thought it would all work itself out. I learned to be a team player in basketball. I learned to hunt and handle being with adults. I had to open myself up to new ideas about how to play from Mr. Schilke. I went to jazz clubs and was exposed to new situations. I had to learn to control my emotions, and I had to learn how to perform in high-pressure situations. But, as I was saying goodbye to Scout, I realized that I'd not done the one thing that Scout gave his life for. I had not respected myself enough to stand up for who I am. Could I have told Mr. Jeffrey and Mr. Hamilton about what was going on?"

Before anyone could answer, the doorbell rang, accompanied by an urgent knocking. Dale jumped up and ran to the door. He opened it to see the red-haired woman from the diner and Jim.

"You must be Dale," she said, holding out her hand.

"Yes, and are you Mrs. Petris, Jim's mom?" he said, returning the handshake. "Won't you come in and sit down? I'll get my parents."

"Dale, who is it?" his mom asked as Dale returned to the dining room.

"It's Mrs. Petris, and she has Jim with her. I didn't know what to do, so I invited them in. They're waiting in the living room."

Mother stood. "Let's see what this is about." Grandmother offered to fix some coffee. "Go on. Grandpa and I will clean up."

Dale followed his parents into the living room, and they introduced themselves.

Standing up, Mrs. Petris shook hands with both of them. "Nice to meet you. Please call me Jean."

The Kingstons offered her and Jim a seat. Mrs. Petris nervously smoothed her skirt. "I want you to know that Jim's behavior has been wrong. If I'd known about this, I would have stopped it. Jim's always been a good boy, but since his father died at the start of the war, he's been defensive and angry at the world."

A look of realization came over Dad's face. "Now I know why I thought I knew the name. Your husband was named Rick, isn't that right? I remember reading about him in the paper after the attack on Pearl Harbor."

Mrs. Petris nodded, her eyes tearing up. "He died aboard the battleship Arizona. But they never recovered his body. They believed he was below decks when the attack occurred just after dawn. We waited several weeks, hoping they could rescue the men below decks, but they never did."

"I'm sorry." Dale's mom said, patting her hand. "I can understand how it would affect a young boy."

"Thank you. I tried to help him understand, but he was never the same. I think he took the anger he felt about his father dying and turned it into intimidating other students. His father played the trumpet, which is the one he plays now. I think he thought that if he weren't the best, he would be letting his father down. It doesn't justify what he did, but at least I've had a chance to give you some of the background, and ... Well, let me have Jim tell you."

Jim, who was sitting next to his mom, leaned forward, his eyes focused on the ground. He popped his knuckles nervously, and then looked directly at Dale and his parents. "First, I want to say I'm sorry for getting Dale suspended and treating him and his friends so badly. My mom and I have talked. I know I have to change my behavior." Jim wiped the tears from his eyes. "I will work hard to regain the respect of all the students and adults I have hurt."

His voice was barely audible as he paused to regain his composure. "Thinking that I caused your dog Scout to die is unforgivable. I realized today that not only did I lose someone I loved, but also I caused someone else to lose someone he loved. I'm so sorry. Can you ever forgive me?" Jim said as he searched Dale's face for a sign of forgiveness.

"Jim, I'm sorry about your dad. If I'd lost my dad in the war, I don't know how I'd react. I'll never understand how you feel, but I do understand that you want to change. I loved Scout," he said, pausing and trying not to become emotional.

"But, Scout would want me to forgive you and move on. We've learned some lessons the hard way." Standing and moving toward Jim, Dale extended his hand.

"Let's work through this together like adults. What do you say?" Jim took Dale's hand, a signal that the past was behind them.

Grandma, who had been listening from the dining room, wiped her eyes and knew it was time for coffee. After some more small talk, Mrs. Petris and Jim left to go home, leaving all to think about what the next day would bring.

Chapter 33

RECONCILIATION

Dale joined his grandfather at the kitchen table the next morning. It seemed strange to him not to be dashing out the door for school on a Tuesday.

He leaned his elbows on the table and sighed. "I feel like a weight has been lifted off my chest. I didn't realize how much I was thinking about Jim and how it had affected me."

Grandfather nodded. "So, what are you going to do for the next four days, since you can't go to school?"

Dale had an idea that he wanted to bounce off Grandfather. After he told him, his grandfather said, "Are you sure you want to do this? I'm not sure the school would approve, and I don't know if your parents would think it's a good idea. Maybe we should wait until they get back from work tonight to discuss it."

"I don't think the school cares what we do while we're suspended. Anyway, it's a way to make this time useful instead of just sitting around and doing nothing."

"Why don't you go for a run and think about it. When you get back, if you still think you want to do it, you can go ahead. We can tell your parents tonight after you see how it goes."

Dale ran out the back door and down the alley, turning on Simpson Hill when Chrissy came out of her house on her way to school.

He ran up to her. "You look nice today. I sure wish I were going to school."

"Thanks! I can't believe what happened in band yesterday. We heard you got suspended. It was the talk of the school about how you flipped Jim on his back. When did you learn to do that?"

"My dad taught me how to defend myself. We've been practicing since September. If you hadn't warned me yesterday, I wouldn't have seen him coming, and it could have been worse."

"I wouldn't let anything happen to you. You know, last night from my window, I swear I could see Jim and his mom in your living room."

"No, you saw right. They came over, and we talked it out. It's a long story, but he's done bullying everyone and wants to earn back the band's respect. He isn't so bad after all."

Chrissy could hardly believe what Dale was saying. "He's been so mean to us that it'll take more than words to gain my trust. Enough talk about Jim … what are you going to do this week, since you can't come to school?"

"I've got some ideas," Dale said vaguely. "You'd better get going so you aren't late. Say hi to the gang." He waved as he ran down Simpson Hill enjoying the morning air. He finished his last lap and paused at the top of the hill overlooking the town of Libertyville. Taking a deep breath, he thought of Scout and decided his earlier idea was the right thing to do. With four days left, it was time to get started.

Chapter 34

CLEARING THE AIR

Dale sat next to Jim in Mr. Hamilton's office with Mr. Jeffrey and Miss Culver, their counselor.

"You two did what? I don't think you should have had any contact while you were suspended."

Dale cleared his throat. "You never said what we could or couldn't do outside of school. I didn't want the time to be wasted." Turning to Mr. Jeffrey, Dale said, "What we did was for the band. The only way to repair the damage was to show that we both have changed. I want the band to hear and see how we worked this out."

"You also involved Sandra. She didn't say anything to me about this," Mr. Jeffrey said.

Jim leaned forward. "That was my idea. I was really mean to her and felt I needed to win her confidence back. We made her promise not to tell. She did it with us after school and on her own time. There's no rule about that, is there."

Mr. Jeffrey said, "I've had some time to think about what has happened. I have some things I want to say to you and the band."

Miss Culver interjected, "From my point of view, I think what they have done is positive and quite grown up. If we could only have all of our school conflicts resolved this way, it would be great."

"Looks like I have to agree," Principal Hamilton said, bringing the meeting to a close. "You may go back to class this morning. I'll look forward to hearing how this turns out."

The boys and Mr. Jeffrey walked down the hall toward the band room. Students and teachers whispered, pointing at the trio as they passed.

"Looks like you have an audience," Mr. Jeffrey acknowledged.

"I think they can't believe we're walking together. I don't think they've ever seen Jim and me together."

"Wait until the band sees us!" Jim said, laughing.

"Let's go in the back door to my office, so the band doesn't see you until you're ready."

"I told Sandra to meet us in your back office earlier today," Dale added.

"So, you were sure that I would let you do this?"

"Jim and I both knew you would let us. We know you are fair and want what is best for the band. This is a way to put the confrontation behind us."

"I hate being so predictable," he said, unlocking the side door.

Sandra was already in the back room when they arrived. "Looks like you convinced him."

"Sure did! Mr. Jeffrey says to wait here until the band plays the introduction to the trumpet trio. You didn't tell the gang about this, did you?"

"No, in fact this morning, I arrived before they did. I didn't even walk to school with them. I wonder what they're thinking."

"Time to find out ... the introduction is starting." Dale buzzed his lips lightly.

As the last note of the introduction ended, Sandra stepped out of the office and played her opening cadenza to *The Three Aces,* causing the band to stare. As she played, she moved to the front of the room, all eyes on her. When she ended, Dale stepped out and played his cadenza to hushed whispers from the band; they watched intently as he strolled over to Sandra.

As Dale finished, the next player, Jim, stepped out from the office and played the final cadenza. When he reached the front of the room, Dale and Sandra joined him for the final phrase, showing they were united as one. They brought down their horns, and the band went wild. When Mr. Jeffrey tapped on his stand for quiet, Dale stepped forward.

"First I want you to know that I'm sorry for disrupting the band rehearsal last week."

Jim moved next to Dale. "I second what Dale said. I hope you see that we've worked out our differences and are ready to move on. I also want you to know I'm really sorry for the way I acted. I was wrong and will do everything I can to earn back your respect. I hope you'll forgive me."

A single clap began, followed by applause from the entire band. Mr. Jeffrey had the trumpeters sit in their section, and he stepped to the podium. It was now his turn.

"I've had a lot to think about after Dale's speech last week. It's hard for me to admit, but I think I was wrong. I was wrong to create the pressure to compete. I created a culture in our band that was toxic and was poisoning our love of music. I had lost what making music is all about, and I got caught up in wanting to win so badly that I failed to see what I was doing to you. I want you to know I will change. With your help, let's find the joy and excitement of making music again without the emphasis on winning at all costs."

Mr. Jeffrey had never revealed so much to his students. As he stood in front of them, they broke the silence with more applause, relieved that the fighting was over.

For the remainder of the rehearsal, the band worked on the concert music with a newly found sense of purpose. After the rehearsal, Dale and his friends talked and shook hands with Jim, sealing the end of the conflict.

Chapter 35

CONCERT

The auditorium was standing-room only for the concert. The two-foot tall golden state trophy would be presented to the school for display in the trophy case outside the auditorium at the concert. The crowd could feel the excitement as the band played each number with more feeling and passion than in previous concerts.

Before the final number and the presentation of the trophy, the brass quintet of Dale, Victor, Sandra, Karl, and P.J. performed the selection that had won the contest. The quintet was backstage waiting to be announced. Dale peered through the curtains and noticed that same tall dark-haired man he had seen at the contest was sitting in the front row, taking notes. Dale leaned over to Sandra.

"Who is that guy? He's been at the holiday concert and both of our contest performances. Now he's here at our spring concert."

"I have no idea, but it's kind of strange he's always around. Who is the other man sitting with him? Looks like they have suitcases with them. In any event, it's our time to play."

The quintet walked onstage to wild applause. When the final note was played, the crowd clapped, giving the group a standing ovation. When the applause died down, Mr. Jeffrey stepped to the mike. Jim, Dale, and Sandra readied their stands for this final number.

"After that last performance, you can see why we won the state trophy. This year has been very exciting for me and the band," he said, turning to the band and smiling. "The three exceptional students you're about to hear opened my eyes to the fact that trophies and contests are not what count. It's the friendships and musical memories we make together that matter in the long run. Trophies gather dust, and those who win them fade from our memories as time goes on. But, what never dies are the memories we have from those performances."

"Our final number will be one of those memories. *The Three Aces* was written by Herbert Clarke to feature three of the world's most famous trumpet players—Del Staigers, Frank Simon, and Walter M. Smith. Tonight, I have a special treat for you and the band's soloists—Jim Petris, Dale Kingston, and Sandra Johanson. So sit back and enjoy." Mr. Jeffrey walked up to the three players and whispered, "After the band's opening phrase, don't play your cadenza right away."

The three players looked puzzled. Jim leaned over to Dale as Mr. Jeffrey went to the podium. "What's he up to?"

"We'll know in a second."

When Mr. Jeffrey raised his baton and gave the downbeat, Dale saw movement from the front row where the two men had been sitting. Dale nudged Sandra and Jim, and with his head, motioned for them to look at the front row. What they saw caused them to pause. The men reached into what Dale originally thought were suitcases, but they were really instrument cases. When they stood, they each held a cornet, glistening in the spotlights.

As the band reached the fermata at the end of the introduction, the two men in unison turned their backs to the band and faced the audience. Mr. Jeffrey gave the cut-off, and the first man played the most amazing cadenza based on the song *Carnival of Venice.* When he finished, the band played the next chord, followed by the second man playing a different cadenza, just as good as the first man, based upon the song *Willow Echoes.*

Just as the cadenza came to a climax, Adrianne stood up and set a case next to the podium. Mr. Jeffrey leaned down, carefully unlatched the case, and took out a gleaming silver cornet. With one hand, Mr. Jeffrey gave the downbeat for the third chord, brought the cornet to his lips, and began to play. Dale recognized this cadenza from one of his etude books, the *Forty-One Studies in Lip Flexibility.* Mr. Schilke had recommended the book.

As Mr. Jeffrey played the final note, the audience jumped to its feet, clapping and shouting, "Bravo!" Mr. Jeffrey had to wait before continuing, which gave him a chance to shout to his three young players. "OK, now you play your parts when I start the band."

Once the applause died down, Mr. Jeffrey started the piece where they had left off, with Jim, Dale, and Sandra playing this time. As the three played, the men came onstage and stood next to them, playing along with them. Jim, Dale, and Sandra had never played better as they tried to match the level of the older players. On the final phrase of the piece, all five players began to *crescendo* to the last note, playing a triad of such magnitude they couldn't believe it. With the crowd on its feet, Mr. Jeffrey gave the cut-off.

The two men turned to Jim, Dale, and Sandra and shook their hands, introducing themselves while the crowd cheered. "I'm Del Staigers, and you must be Dale and Jim," and kissing her hand, he said, "and you must be Sandra." The students were stunned and unable to respond.

The next man introduced himself as Frank Simon, shaking each student's hand before turning to bow to the audience. After several group bows, Mr. Jeffrey asked for quiet and introduced the two men to the audience, followed by another standing ovation.

After the applause died down, Mr. Jeffrey came up to the three students. "This time, I surprised you. You almost gave me a heart attack when you played your ensemble from memory at contest. After you worked out the beginning of *The Three Aces* all by yourselves, I knew I had to do something special."

"But how did you get them to play? We kept seeing the one man at our performances. I think he introduced himself as Del Staigers. Why is he always around, and what was he writing in his notebook?" Dale asked.

"I'll let them tell you. Here they come."

The two men approached and thanked Mr. Jeffrey for the concert. Dale stepped forward to shake Mr. Staigers's hand. "I have just one more question. I've seen you at our performances. Why are you always writing in that little notebook?"

Smiling at Mr. Jeffrey, Mr. Staigers reached into the pocket of his suit coat, pulled out an envelope, and handed it to Dale.

"Rather than explain it, why don't you just read this letter? Then you'll understand."

And with that, the two men left, hurrying down the aisle to catch the last train out of Libertyville.

At the door, Mr. Staigers called back to the students, "If you continue to improve, the future of music is in good hands." Dale squinted into the lights, the envelope unopened in his hands. It had his name and P.J.'s written in ornate script on the front.

Chapter 36

THE LETTER

"Come on! Enough of the suspense!" P.J. said as he slid next to Dale in the empty band room.

"I wanted to wait until it was just us. Let me read the letter first to myself, and then I'll read it aloud to you." He carefully tore open the envelope. The letterhead boldly stated,

National Music Camp
Interlochen, Michigan

Dale smiled as he read the letter. P.J. couldn't wait and grabbed the letter out of Dale's hands. His eyes scanned the page before he proclaimed, "Looks like we're going to be playing music on a lake this summer!"

About the Authors

Paul Kimpton grew up in a musical family and was a band director in Illinois for thirty-four years. He earned a bachelor's and master's degree in music education, and certifications in school guidance/counseling and administration. His father Dale was a high school band director and professor at the University of Illinois, and his mother Barbara was a vocalist. When Paul is not writing, he is reading or enjoying the outdoors.

Ann Kimpton played French horn throughout her college career and went on to be a mother, literacy teacher, and high school administrator. Her parents, Henry and Maryalyce Kaczkowski, both educators, instilled an appreciation of the fine arts and the outdoors in all their children.

Ann and Paul were high school sweethearts who met when they played in the high school band. They have two grown children, Inga and Aaron, who share their love of music, the outdoors, and adventure. Ann and Paul have two grandchildren, Henry and Teagan, who will continue the tradition.

Also available in the *Adventures with Music* series through GIA Publications, Inc. includes the following.

Book 1

Starting Early: A Boy and His Bugle in America During WWII

Book 2

Dog Tags: A Young Musician's Sacrifice During WWII

Book 3

Summer of Firsts: WWII is ending, but the Musical Adventures are Just Beginning

Curriculum Guides are available for all the books in the series.

Coming soon in the *Adventures with Music* series

Book 5

Music on the Lake

Dale and P.J. are invited to the National Music Camp at Interlochen for a summer full of memorable adventures!

For more information, or to contact the authors, please go to adventureswithmusic.net.